Desmond Byrne

Australian Writers

Desmond Byrne

Australian Writers

ISBN/EAN: 9783337313708

Printed in Europe, USA, Canada, Australia, Japan

Cover: Foto ©Andreas Hilbeck / pixelio.de

More available books at **www.hansebooks.com**

AUSTRALIAN WRITERS

AUSTRALIAN WRITERS

BY

DESMOND BYRNE

LONDON
RICHARD BENTLEY AND SON
Publishers in Ordinary to Her Majesty the Queen
1896

CONTENTS.

INTRODUCTION.

Any survey of the work done by Australian authors suggests a question as to what length of time ought to be allowed for the development of distinctive national characteristics in the literature of a young country self-governing to the extent of being a republic in all but name, isolated in position, highly civilised, enjoying all the modern luxuries available to the English-speaking race in older lands, and with a population fully two-thirds native. The common saying that a country cannot be expected to produce literature during the earlier state of its growth is too vague a generalisation. There are circumstances by which its application may be modified. It certainly does not apply with equal force to

1

a country whose early difficulties included race conflicts, war with an external power and political labours of great magnitude, and to another whose commercial and social development, carried on under more modern conditions by a people almost entirely homogeneous, has been facile, unbroken and extraordinarily rapid.

Nor can paucity of literary product, where it exists, be satisfactorily explained by the unrest that continues in a new land long after it has attained material prosperity and the higher refinements of life. The Americans are a type of an extremely restless people. They have been so throughout the greater part of their history, and the characteristic is now more marked than ever. It is a fixed condition of their national being, an expression of the cumulative ambition that is the source of their varied progress. Yet from time to time men have arisen among them who not only have given intimate views of a new civilisation, but have added something to the permanent stock of what Matthew Arnold used to call 'the best that is known and thought in the world.' Even when the independent nationhood of the United States was still but an aspiration, Benjamin Franklin had familiarised Europe with much that has since been recognised as inherent in the modes of thought and manners of the Western race.

The bulk of the literature of America is, of course, still small in proportion to the culture and intellectual energy of the country; but it has been and is sufficient to interpret in a more or less distinctive way all the leading phases in the evolution of the national thought and sentiment. The subtle influence of the deeply - grounded religious feeling which, implanted by the Puritan pioneers, has survived generations of intense absorption in material progress and the distractions that modern life offers to the possessors of newly - acquired wealth; the pride of the people in their independence, and their natural tendency to overrate it in comparison with the conditions of other countries; the contrasts furnished by a society fond of reproducing European habits, yet retaining a simplicity and freshness of its own : these and other features in the progress of the United States for over a century may be found expressed in its literature from the native standpoint, and not merely from that of the intelligent outside observer.

An American writer in discussing, a few years ago, the quality of the literature produced before the War of Secession, when wealth and leisure were abundant among the planters and in the principal New England towns, observed that ' there would seem to be something in the relation of a colony to the mother-country which dooms the thought and art of the former to a hopeless provincialism.' If a comment so largely fanciful could be made respecting Australasia and Canada, it would practically mean—at all events from the American point of view—that as long as they remain dependencies of Great Britain, and therefore lack the stimulus of an active patriotism, so long will much of whatever is individual in their social development and national aspirations be without expression. In the case of the Australasian colonies it would further mean (apart from any consideration of their future independence) that a people far removed from other communities of the same race and already giving promise of being the greatest power south of the equator, must continue for an indefinite period to be wholly sustained and swayed in matters of thought and art by a country over twelve thousand miles distant that happens for the present to offer the most convenient markets in which to buy and sell. The point need hardly be discussed, but it suggests some facts in the intellectual life of Australia that it will be of interest to name. These may not be found to explain why there is yet no sign of the coming of an Antipodean Franklin or Irving, or Hawthorne or Emerson; but they will help to show why the literature of the country grows so unevenly, why it is chiefly of the objective order and leaves large tracts of the life of the people untouched.

Perhaps the paradox that a people may read a great deal and yet not be interested in literature could hardly be applied to the

Australians, but it is a fact that they make no special effort to encourage the growth of a literature of their own. By no means unconscious of their achievements in other directions—in political innovations, in sport and athletics—they appear not to take any pride in or see the advantage of promoting creative intellectual work. Will this be considered natural and reasonable, as already they are supplied with books and plays and pictures from England and Europe, or as a proof of thoughtlessness and neglect? 'Why,' asked a critic in the *Edinburgh Review* in 1819, 'should the Americans write books when a six weeks' passage brings them, in their own tongue, our sense, science, and genius in bales and hogsheads?' Are the Australians of these days asking themselves a similar question? It would seem so. In 1894 they imported books, magazines and newspapers from the United Kingdom to the value of £363,741 : this, too, at a time when most of the colonies were understood to be rigidly economising in consequence of a financial crisis. A decade before the amount was not far short of a hundred thousand pounds higher.

Foremost in his list of the salient intellectual tendencies of the native population of the United States Mr. Bryce places 'a desire to be abreast of the best thought and work of the world everywhere, and to have every form of literature and art adequately represented and excellent of its kind, so that America shall be felt to hold her own among the nations.' And he further attributes to them 'an admiration for literary or scientific eminence, an enthusiasm for anything that can be called genius, with an over-readiness to discover it.'

Artistic talent in America has from an early period in the history of the country enjoyed the stimulus of local respect and attention. Mr. Henry James has testified to the 'extreme honour' in which writers and artists have always been held there. Literature is now a subject of special systematic study in all the important schools; literary organisations are numerous, including no fewer than five thousand circles for the study of Shakespeare; authorship has become something like a craze in fashionable society ; the intelligence of the criticism in the weekly press is on the whole equal to that in English journals; and several of the magazines are largely devoted to the more artistic kinds of writing. If the results of these incentives to production seem comparatively small, as they undoubtedly do, it must not be forgotten that the profession of letters in America long suffered, and is still suffering, from the absence of international copyright law. Before the year 1891 the markets were filled with cheap reprints of British and European works (often of an inferior class), and even now authors have to encounter competition with a vast quantity of foreign matter of which copyright, owing to the peculiar conditions of the law and of the publishing trade, is often obtained at prices much below its real value.

It is not, however, the native literary product of America that is noteworthy so much as the widespread and conscious taste for literature among the people, and the means which they adopt to promote it. The best friend of Australia could not credit it at present with any markedly active desire 'to have every form of literature and art adequately represented and excellent of its kind.' In this respect the results of the high standard of education attained in the Government schools and the subsidised Universities are disappointing. The Universities of Sydney and Melbourne will soon be fifty years old, but neither is yet represented with distinction in the higher forms of literature and art. The Governments, at least, do their duty. Having liberally provided for school education, they spend annually large sums in making additions to picture - galleries, in maintaining libraries (of which there are over eleven hundred), technological schools and museums, and in other ways adding to the comfort and enlightenment of the people. But large private contributions are rare, and the founding or endowment of public institutions still rarer.

Of societies or clubs devoted specially to the interests of literature there are very few—probably not half a dozen. Here and there among the upper classes there are little coteries whose members read the English and French reviews, and are well posted in all movements of interest in the world of letters, but there is no actual organisation among them, and they do not seek to extend their influence. Their ambition is confined to providing for their personal improvement and pleasure. The reading of the people, though extensive, is not serious nor in any way specialised, unless a recent notably high average of borrowing in the historical departments of a few of the free libraries be taken into account. The leading book exporters in London say that throughout the Antipodes the public demand is confined, as in England, mainly to the 'general' literature of the hour. 'Whatever has succeeded in London will usually succeed in Australia' is the invariable remark of the exporter and the first principle that guides his tentative selection in the case of all newly-published works. The circulation of the best British weekly and monthly reviews by some of the principal subscription libraries helps the reader to choose for himself, but if he should wish to buy a new book, however valuable, that has not become popular in the business sense, he will probably have to send to London for it.

The wealthy people seem to select their reading-matter chiefly with a view to entertainment. Not long ago the manager of one of the most fashionable of the Melbourne circulating libraries said that about ninety per cent. of the female and seventy-five per cent. of the male frequenters of such libraries in Australia read only novels. But this average is perhaps rather over-stated, being given at a time when there was an exceptional demand for certain novels that had obtained notoriety by an audacious treatment of sex questions and English society.

A glance at the fare which fourteen of the London publishers provide in their colonial editions. is of interest. Excellent value, of its kind, is usually offered in these issues, but here again we find proclaimed an excessive preference for light prose literature. Of 264 volumes in one 'colonial library,' 238 are of fiction. Sketches, memoirs, reminiscences and a few essays make up most of the balance. The taste of the working classes, so far as it can be ascertained from the records of the principal free libraries, is, curious as it may seem, decidedly sounder than that attributed to the customers of the subscription libraries. It must be remembered, however, that the former are seldom tempted with new fiction, and never with fiction of the spicy or questionable kind. Some of the larger institutions are rigidly exclusive in regard to the light kinds of literature.

Authorship in Australia loses an important incentive in the absence of local magazines. All of the better kind have lacked sufficient public support. Several of them, including the *Colonial Monthly* (established by Marcus Clarke), the *Melbourne Review*, the *Centennial Magazine*, and the *Australasian Critic* (the latter conducted by the professors of the Melbourne University) promised so well that their want of support is not easily explainable. It has been attributed to an unreasoning prejudice, an assumption that being locally produced they must necessarily be inferior ; but this probably does the reading public less than justice. Apparently from their contents, most of the magazines failed because they were made too Australian in character, too unlike the English periodicals to which readers had been so long accustomed. There are many fine magazines in the United States, but their conductors do not make the mistake of trying to do without British and European contributions. They know the value of names as well as of matter. Foreign writers supply about one-third of the contents of the monthlies. When great interest suddenly attaches to some national question, their enterprise, like that of the newspapers of the country, sometimes takes the special form of securing cabled summaries of the opinions of influential politicians in Great Britain and elsewhere for immediate publication.

A contributory cause of the failure of Australian magazines is the fact that the cost of their mechanical production has always been higher than that of any of their imported competitors. This promises to be a difficulty for some years to come. Book-publishing, as a separate business, is also practically impossible, for like reasons. The Australian reader attaches no special value to the possibilities of the local magazine, partly because its place as a literary and art record is considered to be fairly supplied by the weekly newspapers. Moreover, it is said he demands cheapness as well as high quality in his periodicals, and knows that both can be got in several English, American and European magazines. If this be so, the same predilection will no doubt account for the spectacle of leading London firms sending to the colonies tons of their popular modern books in paper covers, and offering them at about half the price charged in the United Kingdom, where they are obtainable only in cloth-bound editions.

That no one has yet lived by the production of literature in Australia is not a matter for surprise. No one, indeed, would seriously think of attempting to do so.

Gordon was a mounted policeman, a horse-breaker, a steeplechase-rider—anything but a professional man of letters ; Marcus Clarke was a journalist and playwright, and wrote only two novels in fourteen years ; Rolf Boldrewood's books were written in spare hours before and after his daily duties as a country magistrate ; Henry Kingsley returned to England before publishing anything ; Kendall held a Government clerkship which he exchanged for journalism ; Mr. Bruton Stephens is in the Queensland Civil Service ; Mr. B. L. Farjeon's colonial work was mainly done in connection with the New Zealand press ; Messrs. Marriott, Watson, E. W. Hornung, J. F. Hogan, Haddon Chambers and Guy Boothby, among younger writers, have taken their talents to London ; and none of the half-dozen female novelists have been dependent upon literature for a livelihood.

What, it may be asked, becomes of the best talent developed by the Australian schools and Universities ? It is employed, or tries to find employment, in the practice of law, medicine, journalism and teaching. From law to politics is but a step in the colonies, and the chances of attaining Cabinet rank, rendered frequent by the prevailing aggressive form of party government, are often attractive to men of ability and ambition. The journalists are more or less drenched with politics all the year round, and they, too, occasionally find it an easy matter to vary their occupation by assisting in the active business of law-making. The tension of their daily lives, severer than that of the majority of press writers in Great Britain, leaves them little or no leisure for literary work of the higher kind, and generally the prospect of being compelled to send whatever they might write to the other end of the world for the chance of publication discourages effort. It may safely be said that there are young men on the editorial and reporting staffs of a dozen of the principal journals who possess ability that would secure them distinction in the wider fields of England or America. To their skill and spirited rivalry is due the universally high quality of the

Antipodean press. Mr. David Christie
Murray, writing after considerable experience of the colonies, and as one who had
been an English journalist, said that on the
whole he was 'compelled to think it by far
and away the best in the world.' The remark is without exaggeration so far as it
applies to the large weekly journals.

The extent of the favour shown by Australian readers to the works of their own
novelists is, as a rule, exactly proportioned
to that which their merits have previously
won in England. Booksellers and their
London agents, who of course treat all literature from a purely commercial standpoint,
are at all events unanimous in discrediting
the existence in recent years of any prejudice
against colonial fiction of the better class. It
is now very seldom sent out in two or three
volume form, they say, but neither are the
most popular English novels, except occasionally to subscription libraries. For representative Australian work, then, there is a
fair field but no favour. It is as though the
function and existence of the authors apart

from the rank and file of English letters were not recognised. There is an exception to this rule in the poet Gordon, as a portion of his writings, the *Bush Ballads and Galloping Rhymes*, irresistibly commemorate the national love of horseflesh and outdoor life. Every Australian now knows that *For the Term of his Natural Life* is a great novel of its class; but as a leading Victorian journalist (Mr. James Smith) once pointed out in an article in the *Melbourne Review*, Clarke's real merit was for years undervalued, because he was known to be 'only a colonial writer.' Thousands of English, European and American readers had admired the novel before they thought of inquiring who the writer was or whence he came. It is true that the story attracted a good deal of interest in Australia even during its first appearance as a serial, but from elsewhere came its recognition as one of the novels of the century.

The authors whose lives and writings are briefly sketched in this volume are all noted in some degree for accuracy and sincerity

in their representation of life in Australia.
They have all written from abundant knowledge—from love, also, perhaps it may be
added — of this great wide land with its
brilliant skies, its opportunities and its wholesome pleasures. That they should fail to
cover their field—that they tell too much of
country life and adventure and too little of
the throb and energy of the cities—is in a
large measure explained by the fact that
their books are of necessity primarily written
for English readers.

Somehow it is assumed that people in
the mother-country continue to be interested
only in the picturesque, the curious and
the unusual in Australian life. The idea
is in part a survival from earlier years
when a host of military officers, Civil Servants, journalists and tourists described in
some form the more obvious peculiarities of
the colonies: their giant, evergreen forests,
strange amorphous animals, aristocratic gold-
diggers, ex-convicts in carriages, and general
state of topsy-turveydom. There is quite an
amazing variety of occasional records of this

class in forgotten books, magazines and
pamphlets. In at least a score of well-
known novels there are charming country
scenes, true in every particular ; but there
is a distinct limit to the power of fiction of
this kind to interest remote readers, while
much repetition of it might well be misleading.

A writer in the *Australasian Critic* once
rightly observed, respecting a batch of short
stories of the conventionally Australian kind,
that English readers might 'fancy from
them that big cities are unknown in Australia ; that the population consists of
squatters, diggers, stock-riders, shepherds
and bushrangers ; that the superior resi-
dences are weatherboard homesteads with
wide verandas, while the inferior ones are huts
and tents.' No foreign reader could understand from them that 'more than half the
Australian population have never seen kan-
garoos or emus outside a zoological garden,
and that not one in a hundred, or even a
thousand, has seen a wild black fellow.'
There is a well-known type of Australian

novel to which the same remarks might apply with almost equal fitness.

The lack of interest on the part of the novelists in the cities is the more noticeable because they contain one-third of the whole population of the country, a proportion said not to have a parallel in any other part of the world. This neglect is surely a mistake, founded on an erroneous conception of the tastes of the English public, and resulting partly from the absence of anything like a local literary influence upon the writers. ' Have the stress and turmoil of a political career no charm ?' asks Mr. Edmund Gosse, in referring to the restricted scope of the English novel, and in making a plea for ' a larger study of life.'

The same question might with very good reason be raised concerning the political life of Australia, which has been almost entirely neglected since Mrs. Campbell Praed used up the best of her early impressions and settled in England. The majority of the writers of fiction who continue to live in the country are women, and possibly

not interested in politics ; but the chief
reason why the romance is seldom written
of the Cabinet Minister who started life
as a gold-digger or draper's assistant, or of
the democratic legislator whose first election
was announced to him through a hole in a
steam-boiler that he was riveting, is to be
found in a belief that it would not be appre-
ciated in the far-off land whither all Australian books must go for the sanction of
their existence.   Here again the British
reader appears to be misjudged, for has he
not accepted from another direction, and
enjoyed, *Democracy* and *Through One Ad-
ministration ?*   Mrs. Praed, lightly skimming
the surface of Antipodean political life in
two of her stories, has shown it to be not
without humour, nor lacking in the elements of more serious interest.   But she
cannot be said to have exhibited any particular belief in the political novel, and
none of the more practised among her
colonial contemporaries has ever given it a
trial.

On the main question of a national literature it will perhaps be concluded that Australia has yet scarcely any need to be concerned : that not much must be expected from a civilisation which, though it has been rapid, began little more than a century ago ; and that the existence of wealth, and the possibilities of leisure and culture which wealth affords, cannot produce the same effect upon art in a new country as in an old one. The whole matter no doubt is somewhat difficult of decision. It has been none the less useful to indicate why so little of the work already done is the work of native writers—why the existence of much of the best of it may almost be considered accidental. And while a refusal to take the trouble of independently judging the worth of a local artistic product may or may not be an invariable characteristic of a new country, it was also right to contradict on the best available authority the assertion of a 'prejudice' against the work of Australian authors.

A portion of the talent that cannot be absorbed in the already overcrowded ranks of law and medicine might find employment in building a literature which should have something of national savour in it, if migration to England were no longer a condition of success to those who would make writing a profession, as migration to New York or Boston is similarly found to be a necessity to the young Canadian man or woman of letters. It need not be wished that the colonial Governments would do more than they have done—certainly not that they would create a sort of civil pension list, as a section of the Legislative Assembly of Victoria contemplated doing ten years ago in discussing a proposed grant to the family of Marcus Clarke. But the Universities might extend their influence, and those who have leisure might combine to introduce some of the methods which have helped to create a living public interest in literature and art in European countries. In other words, there is needed an increased sense of responsibility in the cultured class : those people, among others, who yearly help to fill the luxurious ocean steamships on their long journeys to the Old World, and who bring back so singularly little practical enthusiasm for their own land in the South.

Meanwhile it is encouraging to note the high promise of the work of some of the younger writers. Mary Gaunt (Mrs. H. Lindsay Miller), the daughter of a well-known Victorian judge, has, in *The Moving Finger*, raised the short story to an artistic level hardly approached by any other Australian writer. And Mrs. Alick Macleod, author of *An Australian Girl* and *The Silent Sea*, has given in the former novel—a fine story. despite some irregularities of form —the most perfect description of the peculiar natural features of the country ever written. For the first time the Bush is interpreted as well as described. In the attitude displayed in this story towards the fashionable life of the towns there is habitual impatience and occasional scorn. The sketches of Mrs. Anstey Hobbs' efforts to found a salon, the flirtations of Mrs. Lee-Travers—who 'chose her admirers to suit her style of dress'— Laurette Tareling's solemn respect for

Government House, and the generally
satirical view of the ' incessant mimicking
of other mimicries,' are no doubt justified ;
they are often decidedly entertaining. But
it would of course be a mistake to accept
all this as more than a partial view of Melbourne society. The book does not pretend
to deal with it in other than an incidental
manner. Mrs. Macleod's studies of character
and often clever dialogue suggest that she
might profitably adapt to the presentation of
Australian life the quiet intensity of Tour-
guéneff, or the delicately observant style of
the American critical realists, Henry James,
W. D. Howells and Richard Harding Davis.
And here one wonders whether the Australian novelists who find so little material in
Sydney and Melbourne have seen what the
new writer, Henry B. Fuller, has done with
the life of modern unromantic Chicago ?

According to Mr. Howells, America,
through the medium of its own particular
class of novel, ' is getting represented with
unexampled fulness.' The writers ' excel in
small pieces with three or four figures,' and

are able conveniently to dispense with sensationalism — a point not yet reached by Antipodean novelists. 'Every now and then,' he says, referring to the extreme of this type, 'I read a book with perfect comfort and much exhilaration, whose scenes the average Englishman would gasp in. Nothing happens ; that is, nobody murders or debauches anybody else ; there is no arson or pillage of any sort ; there is not a ghost, or a ravening beast, or a hair-breadth escape, or a shipwreck, or a monster of self-sacrifice, or a lady five thousand years old in the whole story ; " no promenade, no band of music, nossing !" as Mr. Du Maurier's Frenchman said of the meet for a fox-hunt. Yet it is all alive with the keenest interest for those who enjoy the study of individual traits and general conditions as they make themselves known to American experience.' As the Transatlantic social conditions, of which the realistic novel with only three or four figures is understood to be the outcome, are being more or less repeated in Australia, a similar literary medium will probably be found best adapted to the portrayal of life there. At least it may be claimed that there is no lack of material in the shape of individual traits which have not yet been suitably described in any form.

MARCUS CLARKE.

In the peculiarity of his fitful talents, and in
the character of his best work in fiction—a
pathetically slender life's product—Marcus
Clarke is still alone in Australian literature.
Others have shown the cheerful, hopeful,
romantic aspects of the new land ; he, not
less honestly, but with a more concentrated
and individual view, has pictured some of
the monotony of its half-grown society, the
gloom of its scenery, and the painful realities
of its early penal systems. Reputed only as
a novelist, he possessed besides imagination
some of the higher qualities of the critical
historian. And had his life been prolonged,
he might almost have done for Australian
city life what Thackeray did for the London
of seventy years ago. He could, at least,

have written a novel of manners that would
have credited the people of Australia with
some individuality : such a novel as would
mark the effects which comparative isolation
must produce in a people who are educated
and intelligent beyond the average of the
British race, intensely self-contained and
ambitious, and of whom two-thirds are now
native-born,—a novel that would have cor-
rected the too languidly accepted judgments
of omniscient elderly gentlemen, who, after
a few weeks or months spent among the
smallest and most imitative section of Antipodean society, gravely conclude that 'leaves
that grow on one branch of an oak are not
more like leaves that grow upon another,
than the Australian swarm is like the hive
it sprang from.'

A rhetorical half-truth of this kind, as
applied to the entire people, can best be
answered in the manner of the modern
realists. The field is narrow in Australia,
yet not too narrow for the writer who, fore-
going the taste for sensation, will be content
to transcribe and interpret impressions of

the moving humanity around him to their minutest detail ; who will forget the pioneer squatter, the Oxford scholar disguised as a 'rouseabout,' and the digger and bushranger of a past generation ; who will sacrifice something of dramatic effect in the endeavour to produce a faithful and finished picture of colonial middle-class society. As qualifications for such work, Clarke had exceptional courage, straightness of eye, and a decided taste for exposing shams, superadded to a forcible and satirical style of expression.

Whether he had the tact and temperate spirit that must form the basis of these qualities in the production of serious fiction is less certain, if he may be judged by the tone of such minor pieces as *Civilization without Delusion, Beaconsfield's Novels*, and *Democratic Snobbery*. There is a certain violence in these which is more offensive than their undoubted cleverness is admirable or their satire entertaining. They show that the writer retained some of the impetuosity and prejudices which were marked features of his youth.

Clarke was an anti-Semite, therefore in the Beaconsfield novels he saw little beyond an expression of the author's personal exultation as the successful representative of a maligned race. In the theological controversy of *Civilization without Delusion*, an even less effective and becoming performance, the young author revealed a deficiency which, in any writer, can only be regarded as a misfortune and a cause for tolerant regret. The spiritual side of his nature was an undeveloped, almost a barren field. Neglected in boyhood and sapped by early habits of dissipation, it had no strength to resist the agnostic conclusions which were the product in later years of a coldly critical examination of the general grounds of Christian belief.

In dealing with religion, his characteristic independence developed into a stiff intellectual pride, and from that into a recklessness which disregarded alike his public reputation and the feelings of others. But these forays into the preserves of theology were happily rare. Such questions obtained no permanent place in his thoughts : they were only the passing expression of an ever-besetting mental restlessness. It is indeed, surprising that a writer with artistic instinct and a sense of humour should ever have persuaded himself to enter the fruitless field of religious contention at all.

There are a few facts in the early life of Marcus Clarke which are sometimes so strongly, and even painfully, reflected in his brief career that they form a necessary preface to any consideration of his literary work. Soon after his birth at Kensington (London) in 1846 his mother died, and thenceforward through all his youth he seems to have received little advice or attention from relations. His father, a barrister and literary man of retired and eccentric habits, exercised over him a merely nominal authority, and so he had liberty to gratify a spirit of inquiry and curiosity notably beyond his years. At his own home he became the pet of his father's acquaintances, a set of fashionable cynics.

In *Human Repetends*, a sketch of his

published several years later, there is a passage which substantially records his experiences at this time : ' I was thrown, when still a boy, into the society of men thrice my age, and was tolerated as a clever impertinent in all those wicked and witty circles in which virtuous women are conspicuous by their absence. . . . I was suffered at sixteen to ape the vices of sixty. . . . So long as I was reported to be moving only in that set to which my father chose to ally himself, he never cared to inquire how I spent the extravagant allowance which his indifference, rather than his generosity, permitted me to waste. You can guess the result of such a training.'

Left alone in the world at the age of eighteen, upon the death of his father, he emigrated to Australia. Failing to take any interest in a bank-clerkship provided by an uncle for him at Melbourne, he was sent to a sheep-station near Glenorchy, one hundred miles inland. Here again he paid little attention to the occupation chosen for him. All the day and half the night were dreamed away in literary thought. Just as he wandered alone over fern-hill and creek-bed, plain and mountain range, and absorbed impressions of a scenery at once repulsive and fascinating to him, so he dipped into all kinds of literature without method or set purpose. But he preferred fiction, and as the consignee of an endless succession of French novels he became a marked man in the eyes of the village postmaster.

Two years had thus been spent, when a Dr. Lewins, who was known as a 'materialistic philosopher,' visited the station and made the young Englishman's acquaintance. A warm mutual regard resulted, and soon Lewins succeeded in obtaining a small post for Clarke on the Melbourne *Argus*. This was the beginning of the most brilliant journalistic career established on the Australian press.

A less happy result of the same friendship was Clarke's conversion to the arid and uninspiring doctrines of materialism, though perhaps it could hardly be called a conversion in the case of one upon whom the deeper principles of Christian faith had never obtained any real hold.

Colonial democracy seems to have been to Clarke at once a source of inspiration and of scorn. Coming from among the English upper classes, with the education and temperament of an aristocrat, he was yet readily able to sympathise with the higher principles of the new society. Its intelligence, virility and free intercourse broadened and interested him, as it does most young Englishmen. But for that common product of a new country, the pretentious plutocrat, he had only contempt.

It is the bitterness with which this feeling is expressed in his journalistic writings that helps to raise a doubt as to his capacity for work of the best class in fiction. Still, if it be true, as some of those who were his friends say, that this occasional work was seldom much studied, it becomes unreliable as an indicator of the writer's character. The same hand that in the famous *Snob Papers* so savagely, and in at least one case so intemperately, satirised types of English society, afterwards produced novels in which fidelity to the essential facts of life is the most conspicuous quality. So, too, might it have been in the case of the 'Peripatetic Philosopher,' whose weekly criticisms of Melbourne men and manners in 1867-68 has correctly been judged the best writing of its kind yet done in Australia. In these articles, remarkable as the work of one who was only in his twenty-second year, there is a closeness of observation and incisiveness of style which promised much more for their author than the circumstances of his life afterwards permitted him to realise.

The usual effects of an undirected youth and an undisciplined manhood explain Marcus Clarke's failure to render to his adopted country the service which, as a distinctly gifted writer of the realist school, he seemed well fitted to perform. He was a Bohemian, who, while resisting the worst vices of his class, shared its carelessness and improvidence to a degree that left little energy for ambitious work.

His was not an idle nature by any means ;

it was only erratic, fond of variety, impatient of drudgery. Thus, in the course of fourteen years' literary work, his thoughts make excursions from town-life to country-life, from social satire to story-telling, from art to ethnology, from theology to opera-bouffe! Here are the titles of a few of his compositions : *Lower Bohemia in Melbourne* (a sketch), *Plot* (a sensational drama), *Review of Comte and Positive Philosophy* (magazine article), *The Humbug Papers* (humorous and satirical), *The Future Australian Race* (an ethnological study), *Goody Two Shoes* (a pantomime), *Civilization without Delusion* (a theological discussion with the Bishop of Melbourne), *The Power of Love* (an extravaganza), *Doré and Modern Art* (a review), *Cannabis Indica* (a psychological experiment). Almost the whole of Clarke's life may be said to have been devoted to the supply of some temporary demand of the periodical press or the stage. Even the two novels which represent his only sustained work were written for serial issue in Melbourne magazines.

It does not appear in either case that he

wrote with any special view to establish a
literary reputation ; indeed, it would seem
that the story of convict life might not have
been completed but for the strenuous impor-
tunity of the firm of publishers with whom
he had contracted to write it.

Journalism, the early occupation of so
many eminent men of letters, has usually
been abandoned as soon as the young writer
has once shown exceptional ability as a
novelist.   This rule was not followed by
Clarke.   As the leader in his day of the
journalistic class, who, as the late Mr.
Francis Adams has said with substantial
truth, still 'stand almost entirely for the
conscious literary culture of the whole
Antipodean community,' he held a position
which would have unfavourably affected the
literary tone and ambition of a still more
energetic and original writer.

He had no predecessors in the special
work he elected to do ; he had to establish
his own standard of achievement ; and he
was without the constant stimulus which
intercourse with literary society, such as that

of London, affords.   The demands of the
newspapers were then, as now, more for
purely ephemeral criticism or narrative than
for matter worthy to rank as permanent
literature.

An alert, pithy style and a distinct gift of
satirical humour such as Clarke had, and
developed by a wide range of reading, were
just the qualities which are always in request
on the keen, aggressive daily press of
Australia.   One can easily imagine the
flattering demands made upon the young
author's powers by the men who were his
personal friends as well as employers.

Whenever he was deficient in taste of
expression, or in urbanity of criticism (as in
his treatment of the Jews), he showed the
effects partly of impetuous haste, and partly
of his remoteness from those centres of
literary opinion which always beneficially
influence a young writer, be he ever so
original or naturally artistic.   It has been
doubted whether Clarke was ever fully
convinced of his own powers ; but however
feasibly this may have applied to the first

four or five years of his literary career, there
was no ground for it after the unanimously
favourable reception accorded to *For the
Term of his Natural Life* upon its issue in
book form in 1874.

In England and America, as well as in
Australia, this one novel gave him an
immediate and distinct reputation. With
it he might have speedily established himself as one of the leading writers of the day,
and, turning from the depressing realism of
penal cruelties which can have no further
parallel in British countries to something
more within our sympathies—to the realism
of modern Australian life,—have supplied
what is still conspicuously lacking in Australian fiction. Yet, during the remaining seven
years of his life he produced no imaginative
work worthy his name and ability. The
ever-ready market of the local newspaper
press absorbed his best efforts, and such
intervals as there were he devoted to an
attempt to establish himself as a writer and
adapter for the stage.

In this way the years passed without

yielding much beyond a livelihood. Mean-
time, Melbourne was his microcosm : he
made a systematic study of its life from the
purlieus of Little Bourke and Lonsdale
streets to the palace of his 'model legislator' on Eastern Hill. Like Balzac, one
of his favourite novelists, he made observation a severe and regular business, but he
lacked the energy or the patience to take
full advantage of its results. Balzac employed his accumulated materials in bursts
of creative energy which, if terrible in their
intensity and their drain upon his health,
had at least method in them, and effected
their purpose. Poverty did not swerve him,
nor prosperity sate him.

That part of genius which consists in natural
depth and accuracy of vision Clarke had in
abundance, but he was weak in the lesser
gifts of patience and synthetic power, perhaps
also in ambition. Moreover, an unfortunate
extravagance, which led from chronic debt
to bankruptcy, compelled him to continue
the class of work which gave the surest and
most regular income.

Repeated requests by the Messrs. Bentley for more fiction were neglected from year to year, and similar indifference was shown to a flattering invitation to join the staff of the *Daily Telegraph* in London, an opportunity that would have led to the establishment of Clarke in those literary circles outside of which no purely Australian writer, with the exception of Rolf Boldrewood, has ever yet received adequate recognition.

Among Clarke's uncompleted writings are a few brilliant chapters of a novel which promised to be as permanent a record of his ability as the well-known convict story, though of a different kind. But the author had the unlucky faculty of attending to anything rather than the work which offered him certain fame and fortune, as well as the most natural employment of his powers. At the time of his death he was only in his thirty-fifth year. Probably with advancing life he would have become more settled in his tastes and habits, realising that the work at which he was happiest in every sense was the writing of novels, and that alone.

The satire and cynicism so noticeable in Clarke's writings, especially in his critical sketches and essays, are liable to give an inaccurate conception of his temperament. They obscure, as such characteristics nearly always do in literature, the gentler aspects of the writer's nature. His satire is, perhaps, too uncompromising. It often seems to reflect a personal bitterness, to take too little cognisance of the springs of human weakness. Undoubtedly brilliant in force and keenness, it yet too seldom produces the kind of hearty laugh with which Thackeray and Swift, for example, relieve their fiercest scorn. His personal experience of life had been discouraging. He had sounded its depths and sipped its pleasures ; its rude facts found him deficient in self-control and fortitude. He had refused to learn the common logic of existence.

There is an element of tragedy in the rapid change which the unhappy circumstances of his private life wrought in his temperament. Addressing the disciples of Mrs. Grundy in an early essay defending

the Bohemianism of his youth, he tells them
that they are ignorant how easily good spirits,
good digestion, and jolly companions enable
a man to triumph over all the ills that flesh
is heir to. ' You cannot know,' he adds,
' what a fund of humour there is in common
life, and how ridiculous one's shifts and
strugglings appear when viewed through
Bohemian glass. . . . Life seems to you
but as a " twice told tale, vexing the dull ear
of a drowsy man "—seems but as a vale of
tears, a place of mourning, weeping, and
wailing. . . . I wish ye had lived for a
while in " Austin Friars "; it would have
enlarged your hearts, believe me.'

This was the cheerful philosophy of Clarke
as a young bachelor, after he had spent his
slender patrimony, disappointed the successive efforts of friends to make a business
man of him, and was about to begin the
earning of a living by his pen. A dozen
years later we see him with developed
talents and a valuable name, but broken in
fortune and spirit, and gloomily anticipating
death months before it came. The Jew

usurers, whose race he despised, had long
been his real masters, and, with a nature
sensitive in the extreme, he writhed in their
bondage.

Improvidence had been not merely an
unhappy incident, as it is in the lives of so
many young men of artistic tastes ; it had
overweighted him more or less for years,
and 'the thoughtless writer of thoughtful
literature,' as the author of his biographical
memoir has called him, sank beneath it while
yet at the beginning of a career full of the
brightest promise. The sort of companionship that pleased his careless youth had
latterly proved unsatisfying, and to some
extent distasteful to him. Its effects upon
his character were so unfavourable that some
who had been his companions in journalism
felt it necessary, after his death, to credit him
with a greater capacity for kindly forbearance
towards humanity than is apparent in the
bulk of his writings.

'My friend,' says one writer, 'was one of
those many geniuses who appear to be born
to prove the vast amount of contradictory

elements which can exist in the same individual. In his case these contradictions were so apparent—and, if I may use the term, so contradictory — that, unless one knew him, it was impossible to believe what his nature was. On the one hand, he was recklessly generous, impulsively partisan, morbidly sensitive, and highly chivalrous; on the other, forgetful of obligations, defiantly antagonistic, unnecessarily caustic, and affectedly cynical. . . . His life was one of impulse, and the direction of the impulse depended solely on surrounding circumstances. . . . He has passed from us at an early age, leaving behind him some enemies made, perhaps, by his own waywardness; but he has left many friends, too,—friends who loved him for the good that was in him.'

In another sketch of the author, his character is thus summed up: 'Caustic he was sometimes, and cynical always; but beneath there beat a heart of gold—a heart tender and pitiful as a woman's.' This estimate is amply justified by the power of pathos and the often tender analysis of human feeling in *For the Term of his Natural Life*, however absent the same qualities may seem in many of the shorter stories.

An interesting picture of Clarke's personality is given by a writer in the Sydney *Bulletin :* ' His wit was keen and polished, his humour delicate and refined, and his powers of description masterly. . . . His face was a remarkable one—remarkable for its singular beauty. Like Coleridge, the poet, he was "a noticeable man with large grey eyes," and one had but to look into them to perceive at once the light of genius. . . . He was one of the best talkers I have ever met. Like Charles Lamb, he had a stutter which seemed to emphasise and add point to his witticisms. As in his writings, he had the knack of saying brilliant things, and scattering *bons mots* with apparent ease, so that in listening to him one felt the pleasure that is derived from such books as Horace Walpole's correspondence and those of the French memoir-writers. . . . He knew not how to care for money, yet he had none of those vices which ordinarily reduce men of genius to destitution, and are cloaked beneath the hackneyed phrase, " He had no enemy but himself."'

In all his journalistic criticism, Marcus Clarke scarcely more than pointed to the material which the life of such cities as Melbourne and Sydney offer a novelist capable of work like that of Mr. W. D. Howells, or the series of tales of urban society in America by Mr. Marion Crawford. There is now an opportunity, and, one might almost say, a need, for fiction which shall also, in effect, be salutary criticism. The Antipodes have lately illustrated the fact that a single decade will sometimes witness a notable change in the conditions of an entire people in a new and rapidly-developing country.

Thus, with the struggle for subsistence now keen to a degree which could not have been foretold by the gloomiest pessimist a few years ago ; with Parliaments, hitherto safely democratic, threatened with Socialism by the increasing practice of electing artisans and labourers to do the legislative work of their respective classes ; the crash of fortunes which never had substantial existence ; the pauperising to-day of the paper millionaire of yesterday ; the spectacle of worn, old men, after overreaching and ruining themselves, starting pitifully the race of life afresh, a sinister experience their sole advantage over the faltering novice ; and that other common spectacle of democratic life, the secure and cultured rich cynically eschewing the active business of government,—with these and some social aspects still less agree able to contemplate there is ample subject-matter for any novelist who may have the disposition and ability to carry on the work which Clarke had indicated, but scarcely begun, before he died.

Long Odds, Clarke's first story, deals with English life, and bears no resemblance in quality or kind to the later novel with which his name is chiefly associated. It is primarily the tragedy of a *mésalliance*, and horseracing and politics assist the plot, with the usual complications of gambling and

intrigue. The story has, however, a good
deal less to do with sport than the title
suggests. The plot is mainly concerned
with the selfish, cruel, and infamous in
human nature—a singularly dark theme for
a young beginner in fiction to choose.
Except at rare intervals when the business
of characterisation is momentarily set aside,
as in the vivid descriptions of the Kirk-
minster Steeplechase and the Matcham Hunt,
there is little suggestion of youthful spirit or
freshness.

The outlines of plot and incident are
attractively arranged, the expression of life
for the most part second-hand and artificial.
There are traces of Dickens' burlesque without his sympathy, and the high colouring
of Lytton with less than Lytton's wit.
Disraeli's satire, too, is echoed in the political
scenes. The young Australian squatter, whose
experiences in England were to have formed
the main purpose of the book, is allowed no
opportunity to show the better, and rarely
even the ordinary, capabilities of the new
race of which he is ostensibly a type.

It is said to be a well-understood maxim of the novelist's art that many a liberty taken with hero or heroine, or both, is forgiven if the writer keeps a constant eye upon his villain, and deals honestly by him. In *Long Odds* there are two villains, and at least two others villainously inclined. Between the four of them the easy-going hero has no chance.

It is natural that, in the construction of a novel which aims at dramatic point before anything else, the ' simple Australian,' as his author is at last constrained to regard him, should seem less useful than the polished and unprincipled man of the world. But in this instance the balance of interest is too unequal. Dramatic quality has been secured at the expense of tone and proportion. Of the two male characters whose exploits in rascality it becomes the real business of the story to tell, Rupert Dacre is the more natural and entertaining.

There is an attention to detail in his portrait which suggests that the lineaments of the conventional society villain may have been filled in with the help of a little personal knowledge, perhaps of some of those morally doubtful individuals already mentioned as having been among the acquaintances of Clarke's early youth. Dacre is the chief cynic of the story, and to him are assigned the best of the dialogue and all of the small stock of humour to be found in the novel. But the man who is both his associate and enemy, Cyril Chatteris, is a common sort of dastard, and altogether disagreeable.

The author is not entirely forgetful of the interests of his nominal hero. If throughout three-fourths of the story Calverley is made the plaything of circumstances that favour only rogues, he is at last allowed a triumph in love and sport which, though unsatisfying from an artistic point of view, is calculated to soothe a not too fastidious taste for poetic justice.

Conscious of the conventional character of his principal theme, the author apparently sought to improve it by deepening its intensity. The result of this was to add more of weakness than of strength. Incidents that might have been effectively dramatic become melodramatic ; the conceivably probable is sometimes strained into the obviously improbable. The agreeable finish to the minor love-story of Calverley and Miss Ffrench does not remove the general savour of sordidness which the reader carries away from the study of so much of the bad side of human nature.

In connection with criticism of this kind, it ought, however, to be noted that other hands besides the author's are known to have contributed to the novel. Shortly after it began to appear serially in the *Colonial Monthly*, Marcus Clarke fell from a horse while hunting, and sustained a fracture of the skull which interrupted his literary work for many weeks. How much of the writing had previously been done seems to be a subject of dispute. It is, however, quite clear that, in order to preserve continuity in the publication of the parts, Clarke's friends did write some portion of the story, but whether in accordance with the author's *scenario*, supposing one to have existed, has not been stated.

'Only a few of the first chapters' were
the work of Clarke, says the editor of the
Marcus Clarke Memorial Volume, writing
in 1884; but in an article published in the
Imperial Review (Melbourne) for 1886, the
contributed matter is limited to a couple of
chapters written by Mr. G. A. Walstab, and
skilfully inserted in the middle of the novel.
Walstab was one of Clarke's best friends, and
he is no doubt the 'G. A. W.' to whom the
story is dedicated 'in grateful remembrance
of the months of July and August, 1868.'

From the absence of a prefatory explanation when *Long Odds* was published in
book form in 1869, it may be assumed that
Clarke was satisfied with the quality of the
contributed work. At least, he was willing
to take the full responsibility of its authorship. But even with this in view, it were
well, perhaps, not to hold him too strictly
accountable for the faults of the story. Not
much must be expected from a first novel
produced in the circumstances mentioned, and
issued when the author was only twenty-
three. In his haste to give it final shape

immediately after the serial publication, he was probably ill advised. One can only regret that it was not set aside for a year or so, and written afresh, or, at least, largely revised. Perhaps this would have been expecting too much from so unmethodical a worker as Clarke. The far finer dramatic taste and literary form of his masterpiece, issued five years later, showed how little indicative of his talent was the earlier work.

In view of the large extent to which the life of the Australian landed classes has been described in fiction during the last twenty years, it is curious to read the plea Clarke offered to his Antipodean critics for passing over the literary material close at hand and preferring the well-worn paths of the English novelist.

During the serial publication of *Long Odds* the colonial press raised some objection to the laying of the scene in England instead of in Australia. The author replied simply that Henry Kingsley's *Geoffry Hamlyn* being the best Australian novel that had been, or probably would be, written, 'any attempt to paint the ordinary squatting life of the colonies could not fail to challenge unfavourable comparison with that admirable story.'

The excuse is just a little too adventitious to have convinced even those to whom it was originally addressed. None the less, it may at the moment have accurately represented the opinion of a beginner who at that time could scarcely have known the extent of his own powers.

Probably he had given the subject little thought. His colonial experience was certainly less varied than Kingsley's had been. Above all, his tastes, and in some degree his temperament, differed markedly from those of his predecessor in the field. The judgment or instinct that kept him from coming into direct competition with Kingsley—assuming his own questionable belief that any effort of his would have been competition—at least erred on the side of safety. That the immediate alternative should have been an imitative example of a hackneyed

class of English novel, ineffective of purpose,
book-inspired, and tainted with the deadness
of cynicism, is something which admits of a
more definite opinion.

'I have often thought,' says the writer,
referring to the hero of *Geoffry Hamlyn*
'and I dare say other Australian readers
have thought also, How would Sam Buckley
get on in England? My excuse, therefore,
in offering to the Australian public a novel
in which the plot, the sympathies, the interest, and the moral, are all English, must
be that I have endeavoured to depict with
such skill as is permitted to me the fortunes
of a young Australian in that country which
young Australians still call " Home." '

Without this prefatory sign-post, the reader
could never have suspected such a purpose.
Clarke may have had it definitely in his mind
when he first sat down to the work ; but if
so, it was put aside, consciously or unconsciously, after the completion of the first few
chapters, in favour of more complex characterisation.   Bob Calverley, the young
squatter, really holds a third or fourth place

in relation to the main motive of the story, and is used rather as a foil than as an exemplar of anything typically Australian. He does not bear any active part in the drama of passion and intrigue ; he is not even permitted to be a passive spectator of it.

To say that he was good-natured, jovial, popular, 'the sort of man that one involuntarily addresses by his Christian name' ; that although he was shy and awkward in the society of ladies, at ease with his own sex only when cattle and horses were the subject of conversation, ignorant of music, and unable to tell Millais from Tenniel, he 'could pick you out any bullock in a herd . . . shear a hundred sheep a day . . . and drive four horses down a sidling in a Gippsland range with any man in Australia,'—to say all this by way of preliminary, to add that Calverley was no fool, and yet to show him in scarcely any other guise than that of a trusting victim of rogues, is to go a very short distance in the portrayal of a typical Australian.

In the slack-baked condition in which we find him, he merely repeats the ordinary spectacle of green youth in the process of seeing life and buying experience at the usual high figure. Compared with the real squatter (who, ordinarily, is college-trained, and does not shear sheep nor risk his neck unnecessarily), Bob, the son of rich 'Old Calverley,' and nephew of an English baronet, is as an exaggerated stock-figure of the stage to the commonplace blood and brain of every-day life. A childlike trust in one's fellows, a reputation for good-nature, an untamable taste for horseflesh and the pursuits of the Bush, belong to every young squatter in a certain class of Australian fiction; they are qualities which may be applied indiscriminately, with always some effect.

The real squatter is a more civilised and reliable, if less picturesque, person. He likes both work and pleasure, provided they be suitably proportioned. His work is in the personal management of his properties; his pleasure is taken in the large cities. He entertains no fantastic prejudices against urban life, in proof of which he often spends his later years in some city hundreds of miles from the scene of his early toil and pastoral successes.

As a young man in London, he can be found with rooms at the Langham, the Métropole, or some other of the half-dozen fashionable hotels known to colonial visitors. There he will entertain his friends, joining with them, in turn, the continuous movements of the society season. He frankly lacks much of the ease and polish of the young Englishman, but his natural amiability and good spirits largely compensate for these deficiencies, while they preclude any feeling of discomfort on his own part.

During his three or six months' stay in London (the combination usually of a little business with a very full programme of pleasure) he spends freely, and in his tour of the clubs plays here and there a little at cards—perchance loses. Worldly beyond his reputation, and somewhat Chesterfieldian in his principles, he consents to be a Roman while at Rome. He has inherited the British hatred of fuss and personal peculiarity, and none shall call him mean. But, unlike many of his English friends at club and course, he has watched and taken some part in the hard process of making money, and knows the difference between a little gentlemanly extravagance and the reckless hazarding of a fortune. At least, it may be affirmed of him that in nine cases out of ten he is decidedly no fool.

These are only a few of the prominent outlines of the type of young man who, his holiday over, returns unspoiled to work on his own or his father's estates. Those whose passion for a horse destroys all self-control, who spend thousands in gambling and betting, who innocently take every smooth gentleman at his own valuation, are merely individuals —persons who may as unfailingly be found in England or elsewhere as in Australia.

Sam Buckley is a typical descendant of the British pioneer colonists, as every Australian knows. In attempting to give an answer to his own speculation of ' How would Sam Buckley get on in England?' Clarke presumably undertook to continue the portrayal of this type. The result, considered apart from the function Calverley fulfils in *Long Odds*, must be held as emphatically a failure.

Never was a novel written with a franker or more deliberate purpose than that shown in *For the Term of his Natural Life*. The author had the twofold object of picturing the dreadful crudities and brutalities of the early system of convict 'reformation' in Australia, and of preventing their possible repetition elsewhere. The first of these aims was attained with a fuller employment, and perhaps more moderate statement of historical facts, than can be found in any other fiction of the same class ; the second was ineffective, because, when it found expression, the abuses which had suggested it no longer continued at the Antipodes, and could not conceivably be repeated on the existing settlements at Port Blair and Noumea.

The story was written a quarter of a century too late to assist the abolition of convict transportation to Australia. Had it appeared at the right time, it might have done much where formal inquiries and the

testimonies of disinterested and humane
observers had repeatedly failed.   For sixty
years the practice of deporting criminals had
been carried on, upheld in England by
official indifference and callousness, and in
the colonies themselves by the greed of a
small class of private persons who grew
rapidly wealthy upon the strength of assigned
convict labour, until the free emigrants by
the authority of their numbers were able to
insist upon its cessation.   For so long as the
colonies were willing to receive a population
of criminals, so long was England only too
anxious to supply them and make a virtue
out of it.   It mattered little to the official
mind that the system was incurably bad and
immoral ; the main thing was to speedily and
effectually transfer an awkward burden to
other shoulders.   The entire history of penal
transportation from Great Britain throws a
sinister light upon the national character.
The practice originated with banishment of
convicts to the American colonies under
conditions which constituted a form of
slavery.

The criminal on being sentenced became a marketable chattel of the State. His services were sold by public auction, the purchaser acquiring the right to transport him and sell him for the term of his sentence to a builder, planter, manufacturer, or other employer beyond the Atlantic. The price paid to the British Government averaged five pounds per head, and some of the more useful prisoners were resold in America for twenty-five pounds each. One of these dealers in convict labour, in giving evidence before a committee of the House of Commons, made a matter-of-fact complaint that 'the trade' was not so remunerative as people supposed. Artisans sold well, but the profit realised upon them was often consumed by losses upon some of the others. One-seventh of his purchases died on his hands, and in the course of business he had been obliged to give the old, the halt and the lame in for nothing. When the War of Independence closed the United States against the traffic, Britain was given a fresh opportunity to reconsider and place its penal system upon a more humane basis ; but the temptation to adopt sweeping measures was once more too strong to be resisted. The promoters of the Australian scheme were in so great a hurry to seize their chance that they despatched over seven hundred convicts before even the site for the first settlement was chosen. The hardships which this characteristic act afterwards entailed are too familiar in history to need repetition. After such recklessness, it is no wonder that, as Sir Roger Therry has observed, 'the first-fruits of the system exhibited a state of society in New South Wales which the world might be challenged to surpass in depravity.'

A generation passed before the British Government reluctantly admitted transportation to be a failure. Lord John Russell, as late as 1847, discovered that it had been 'too much the custom to consult the convenience of Great Britain by getting rid of persons of evil habits, and to take that view alone.' In planting provinces which might become empires, they 'should endeavour to make them, not seats of malefactors and convicts, but communities which may set examples of virtue and happiness.'

This mild, platitudinous rebuke came when all the damage was done. It remained for the free inhabitants of Australia to point to a plainer principle in declaring that 'the inundating of feeble and dependent colonies with the criminals of the parent State is opposed to that arrangement of Providence by which the virtue of each community is destined to combat its own vice.'

To illustrate in a single story all the most prominent and pernicious features of the transportation system, Clarke had to invent a case of crime in which the criminal, unlike the majority of the worst offenders sent to the settlements, should always be worthy of the reader's sympathy. It was necessary that the felon be a victim as well as a felon ; that he should not regain his liberty in any form, but continue by a series of offences against the authority of his gaolers to experience and display all the successive severities of Macquarie Harbour, Port Arthur, and Norfolk Island. A fundamental fact to be exhibited was the impassable gulf of misunderstanding that might exist between capricious or incompetent prison officials and a criminal who, for any reason, had once come to be regarded as hopelessly vicious. 'We must treat brutes like brutes,' says the prime martinet of the story : 'keep 'em down, sir ; make 'em *feel* what they are. They're here to work, sir. If they won't work, flog 'em until they will. If they work —why, a taste of the cat now and then keeps 'em in mind of what they may expect if they get lazy.'

The author chose to represent the extreme case of a man who, innocent of a murder charged against him, allowed himself to be transported under an assumed name in order to prevent the exposure of a long-concealed act of unfaithfulness on the part of a beloved mother.

Richard Devine is the bastard son of an aristocratic Englishwoman who in early youth was forced by her father into a loveless union with a rich plebeian. The single fault of the mother's life is confessed after twenty years.

when the husband in a moment of anger strikes her high-spirited and obstinate son. The latter consents to leave his home for ever, and relinquish the name he has borne. On these terms the wife is spared. Richard Devine goes on the instant. Crossing Hampstead Heath, he comes upon a robbed and murdered man, and presently is arrested for the crime. The explanation that would save him would also cause the dreaded exposure of his mother, and so he withholds it, gives a false name, and, having put himself beyond the means of defence and the recognition of friends, is convicted and sentenced to transportation for life.

In making all the subsequent career of Rufus Dawes abnormally painful—that of a dumb sufferer who in sixteen years' confinement, ending only in a tragic death, experiences by turns every form of punishment and oppression—the author often touches, though it cannot be said he ever exceeds, the limits of possibility.

' Need one who was not a hardened criminal have suffered so much and so long ?'

is the question that continually recurs to the
mind of the reader ; but it is suggested by
the prolonged and pitiful sense of unsatisfied
justice rather than by any doubting that the
extremes of penal discipline as practised in
the name of the British Government between
forty and sixty years ago could have been
successively applied to a single human being.
The writer adheres relentlessly to his central
idea to the end.   Dawes' unameliorated
servitude and unavenged fate were intended
to symbolise glaring anomalies of justice
which never were remedied.   The ' correc-
tion ' he is subjected to was that which the
laws of the time permitted, and which in
many cases goaded its victims to draw lots
to murder one another in order to escape
from their misery.

Some of the least creditable features of
convict transportation, of which it was said
by Earl Grey in 1857 that their existence
had been a disgrace to the nation, came to
an end only when the system itself was
abolished.   But novelist and statesman alike
struck at the abuses without feeling it neces-

sary to mention any of the good results of
the system. Its inherent merits were strictly
few, indeed ; yet they ought to be sought in
history by anyone who would get a fair idea
of the prison policy of the period. It is, of
course, inevitable that the criticism conveyed
in a strong imaginative work should fail to
give a full view of results so complex as
those produced by the largely haphazard
method of the Australian penal settlements.

The practice of assigning prisoners to
private employment, for example, produced
notable effects upon society, of which Marcus
Clarke's story gives but the faintest indication.
If Rufus Dawes had been an ordinary first
offender, he might have regained liberty
soon after his arrival in Van Diemen's Land.
But, as we have seen, it was the purpose of
the author to make him exhibit all the rigours
of convict discipline. His case must therefore be regarded as more exceptional than
typical. As a rule, only men inveterate in
crime were detained in constant punishment.
Transportation for life meant servitude only
for eight years if the convict conducted him-

self well, a condition which, of course, depended largely on the sort of master who secured his services. Major de Winton, an officer who served for some years on Norfolk Island, has mentioned that a prisoner by good conduct received a ticket-of-leave after he had been twice sentenced to death, thrice to transportation for life, and to cumulative periods of punishment amounting to over a hundred years!

An interesting view of Marcus Clarke as a literary workman is obtained from the story of the conception and laborious writing of *For the Term of his Natural Life*. It affords the first, and unhappily the last, evidence of how far he recognised the claims of realism in fiction ; and from the account of his suffering under the self-imposed drudgery of keeping to the strict line of history, we see the man as his friends knew him contrasted with the conscientious artist known to the general reader of his famous novel.

The best of Clarke's minor writings display the results of much general culture, but give no proof of special preparation. They are short, concentrated, forcible—the natural expression of a brilliant, impetuous, and spasmodic worker. He overcame his natural repugnance to lengthened toil and minute thoroughness when he saw them to be essential conditions of his task. But the effort was a severe one.

In 1871, when about twenty-five years of age, he was ordered to recruit his health by a trip to Tasmania. He had been for over three years writing extensively for the press, and joining in the gaieties of Melbourne life at a rate which a constitution much stronger than his could not have withstood. The idea of writing a story of prison life had suggested itself previously during his reading of Australian history. Finding himself now without sufficient money for the proposed holiday, he decided to put into active progress this literary project which had hitherto been only vaguely outlined.

Printed records of the convict days there were in abundance at Melbourne, and from these alone such a writer could have made a sufficiently striking story. But he concluded

that he could make his picture at once truer
and more vivid when the surroundings of
the old settlements had become a full reality
to his mind. Messrs. Clarson, Massina and
Co. readily contracted with the young novelist
for the first publication of the story in their
monthly, the *Australian Journal,* and made
him an advance of money. Off he went
with characteristic confidence, and some weeks
later returned ready primed and eager for
the new work. His enthusiasm soon cooled.
The story commenced to appear after the
first few chapters were written, and the unbroken industry necessary to maintain a
regular supply of the parts was more than
Clarke could give.

Writing against time, he is said to have
felt like a convict himself. The irregular
dribbling out of the story so injured the
reputation of the journal that for a time its
circulation was reduced to one - half the
ordinary issue.

Mr. Hamilton Mackinnon, the writer of a
sympathetic memoir of Clarke, has given an
entertaining account of what followed : ' The

author would be frequently interviewed by the publishers, and would as frequently promise the copy. When moral suasion was apparently powerless to effect the required object, payments in advance were made with somewhat better results ; but as this could not go on *ad libitum*, copy would fall into arrears again. At last it was found that the only way to get the author to finish his tale was to induce him into a room in the publishing-house, where, under the benign influences of a pipe, etc., and a lock on the door, the necessary work would be done by the facile pen ; and in such manner was *His Natural Life* produced.'

In a note of apology to their readers in January, 1871, the publishers print a somewhat comical letter which they had received from the delinquent author. Forwarding a single chapter of the story, he tells them that they must make shift with it as best they can, and he will let them have a larger supply during the following month. The letter concludes nonchalantly as follows : 'This is awkward, I admit, and I suppose some good-natured friend or other will say that I have over-plum-puddinged or hot-whiskied myself in honour of the so-called festive season, but I can't help it.'

The story as first published was much longer than the form in which it appears in the English edition. At the request of the present writer, Sir Charles Gavan Duffy, who was one of Clarke's literary friends, supplies the following account of how the novel came to be so extensively curtailed :

'As one of the trustees to the public library (Melbourne), I saw Clarke constantly, and had always a friendly, and sometimes a confidential, conversation with him. He visited me now and then at Sorrento, and on one of these occasions he spoke of a story he had running through a Melbourne periodical about which he was perplexed. He asked me to read it, and tell him un-reservedly what I thought of it. I read the story carefully, making notes on the margin, and wrote him frankly the impression it had made on me.

'After twenty years I can recall the substance of the letter, which is probably still in existence. A powerful story, I said, but painful as it is powerful. The incidents, instead of being depressing, would be tragic if they befell anyone we loved or honoured. But there was no one in the story whom he could have intended us to love or honour. The hero underwent a lifelong torture without any credible, or even intelligible, motive, and on the whole was a *mauvais sujet* himself. To win the reader's sympathy, all this must be altered. I strongly advised that the latter part of the story, in which the Ballarat outbreak was described under a leader whom he named Peter Brawler, should be omitted ; and I objected to the publication of a song in French *argot* with a spirited translation, as the latter would naturally be attributed to the author of the novel, whereas I had read it in an early *Blackwood* before he was born.

'Marcus Clarke thanked me warmly, and said he would adopt all my suggestions. He wrote a new prologue, in which he made the protection of his mother's good name the motive of the hero's silence, and he omitted both the things I had objected to.'

Ending, as it began, with a tragedy, the artistic unity of the novel is thus preserved, and the dominant aim of the author emphasised. Many of those who read it in the serial parts strongly disapproved of the excisions, but there can be little doubt that the story is the stronger for their having been made.

It was as the work of a vivid historian, rather than of a social reformer, that Marcus Clarke's masterpiece won its popularity, and, for its dramatic and substantially accurate view of the worst (always the worst) aspect of convict life, it will continue to be read while anyone remains to take an interest in the unhappiest period of Australian history. From its pages may be learned how long it has taken the intelligent theorist of the British Government to acquire a practical method of treating a difficult social question; how long stupidity and inhumanity may be practised with the sanction of what Major Vickers was fond of respectfully calling ' the

King's regulations'; and how far English
gentlemen, remote from the influence of
public opinion and invested with more power
than single individuals should ever possess,
may become despots, and even blackguards.

It is a grim record. Let those who are
inclined to doubt it turn to the originals,
especially to the report of the House of
Commons Committee of 1837-38, and they
will find facts which the creator of Rufus
Dawes, with all his supple fancy and delicacy
of language, could not bring himself even to
indicate. There are episodes which the more
matter-of-fact historians barely mention, but
do not take advantage of their great privileges to describe. For example, there were
times during the first thirty years of the
century when the open and general lewdness
of the officials on some of the principal
settlements, in their relations with the female
convicts, rendered them totally unfit for the
positions they held.

Clarke in his researches obtained abundant
knowledge of this, but made no use of it
save in adding a few luminous touches to his

portrait of Dawes' passionate and licentious cousin.

In reading the novel for its historical interest, it is necessary throughout to remember the limitation that the writer has specifically put upon himself. He did not undertake to illustrate any of the good effects of exile upon a section of the first offenders sent to the colonies, and scarcely touches the travesties of justice so often wrought by that lottery in human life known as the assignment system. His purpose is to describe 'the dismal condition of a felon during his term of transportation,' and to show the futility of a prison system loosely planned at one end of the world and roughly executed at the other by men who found it easier, and in some cases more agreeable, to their undiscerning hearts to coerce than to ameliorate.

The Parliamentary Committee defined transportation as 'a series of punishments embracing every degree of human suffering, from the lowest, consisting of a slight restraint upon freedom of action, to the highest, consisting of long and tedious torture.' It was with the latter part of the definition in mind that Clarke told his story. He chose to represent servitude in the chain-gangs of Van Diemen's Land and Norfolk Island as the condition of slavery which Sir Richard Bourke and Sir George Arthur admitted it to be, as the utter failure described by the experienced Dr. Ullathorne, and as the system recommended by the House of Commons Committee to be abolished as incapable of improvement and 'remarkably efficient, not in reforming, but still further corrupting those who undergo punishment.'

The idea which is the ganglion of Clarke's plot was always seen clearly, but never obsessed his mind as did a cognate theme that of the impetuous reformer Charles Reade. In his crusade against the form of punishment known as the 'silent system,' the English novelist obtrudes his moral with a frequency that weakens the effect of his often splendid eloquence. The direct opposite of this style is seen in the Australian novel.

The author never openly preaches. His best effects are obtained by quiet satire conveyed in the gradual limning of his characters, and by occasional incidents of which each is allowed to give its own lesson to the reader. The facts have all the advantage of a studiously calm and impersonal presentation.

In the rapid progress of the plot the reader is kept keenly interested. If he have an eye for the moral he will detect it at once ; if not, there is no importunate author to force it upon him. In either case he will find the story an absorbing one. 'It has all the solemn ghastliness of truth,' said Lord Rosebery, writing to the novelist's widow in 1884. He confessed that the book had a fascination for him. Not once or twice, but many times, had he read it, and during his visit to Australia he spent some time in viewing the scene of the old settlements and examining the reports upon which the novel is so largely based.

That there are some exaggerations in the treatment of facts need hardly be stated, but they are few in number, not serious in import,

and outbalanced by numerous cases in which
it has been necessary to modify the description
of incidents either too painful or horrible to
be fully depicted. As a compensation for its
occasional storical inaccuracy, *His Natural
Life* is notably free of the melodramatic
excesses that most young writers would have
been tempted to commit. Clarke was too
good an artist to think of pleading the
sanction of facts for any misuse of the
privileges of good fiction. To maintain a
strong impression on the reader, his touch is
occasionally strong and fearless, like that of
Kipling. But this object attained, he uses
his materials with an almost unnecessary
reticence. The episode of the cannibalism
of Gabbett and his fellow-convicts is exceptional. Yet it purposely falls short of the
terrible original, which is happily hidden
away from general view between the covers
of an old Parliamentary report.

It has been said of Clarke, by one of his
friends, that in his estimate of motives he was
invariably cynical. Though the assertion
goes too far, it seems to suggest the best

explanation of his notable preference for
delineating the dark side of human nature.
He appeared ever to see vice more clearly,
or at any rate to find it more interesting for
the purposes of fiction, than the good or the
neutral in character. But his cynicism—if it
really formed a settled feature of his character
—was not of the kind that implies any indifference to injustice or dishonesty. In this
particular, both his fiction and essays have no
uncertain tone. It is indeed a fault of Clarke
that his bad characters are in most cases
wholly bad. He makes Frere abandon a
life of debauchery under the influence of a
pure woman's affection, but the effect is
afterwards destroyed by evidences that the
attachment on the man's side is sensual and
based on vanity. Moreover, Frere the prison
tyrant and base denier of Dawes' heroism
remains unexcused.

Bob Calverley and Miss Ffrench, the only
important representatives of the ordinary
virtues in *Long Odds*, are little more than
dim shadows contrasted with the clearly-
marked personalities of half a dozen others

in the story who are rogues, or the associates and instruments of rogues. 'The human anguish of every page' of *His Natural Life* which Lord Rosebery found so compelling to his attention, need not have been so continuous and unqualified.

The author seems purposely to have ignored the opportunity afforded by the story for the introduction of a character who, while asserting the claims of Rufus Dawes and the broader interests of humanity, need not have defeated the main motive of the plot. It was a decided error not to gratify in this way the combative instinct of the reader. The Rev. James North—'gentleman, scholar, and Christian priest'—might have been an active opponent of cruelty like Eden, the clergyman in *It's Never Too Late to Mend*, instead of being made a pitiable example of a confirmed and self-accusing drunkard.

The strength of *His Natural Life* lies not so much in the ingenuity and dramatic quality of its plot, as in the number of striking personalities among its leading characters. That of Rufus Dawes, curiously, is distinct only at intervals. It represents, for the most part, a hopeless sufferer passing through a series of punishments which become almost monotonous in their unvaried severity.

But what could be more luminous than the portrait of Sarah Purfoy, the clever, self-possessed adventuress with the single redeeming quality of an invincible love for her worthless and villainous convict-husband? or that of Frere, the swaggering, red-whiskered, coarsely good-humoured convict-driver, glorying in his knowledge of the heights and depths of criminal ingenuity and vice, and frankly ignorant of all else?

How naturally from such a person comes that savagely humorous dissertation upon the treatment of prisoners! 'There is a sort of satisfaction to me, by George! in keeping the scoundrels in order. I like to see the fellows' eyes glint at you as you walk past 'em. Gad! they'd tear me to pieces if they dared, some of 'em.'

Frere is a triumph of consistent literary portraiture. He is generally understood to have been a study from life. But as the

official whose name has sometimes been associated with the character was a considerably
more humane disciplinarian than the perse-
cutor of Rufus Dawes, it must be assumed
that Clarke aimed only at the representation
of a type.

Brutes like Frere and his vindictive associates, Burgess and Troke, there undoubtedly
were on the settlements, but the average
official has probably a better representative
in Major Vickers, the Commandant. Vickers
is not an unkind man, but does not trust
himself to do anything unprovided for in
the 'regulations,' for which he has an abject
respect. 'It is not for me to find fault with
the system,' he says; 'but I have sometimes
wondered if kindness would not succeed
better than the chain-gang and the cat.'
But he never gives intelligence, much less
kindness, a fair trial.

Sylvia Vickers is the only complete picture
of a good woman to be found in any of the
author's stories. Taken in childhood by her
parents to the penal settlements, and separated there for years from youthful society,

familiarised with the constant aspects of crime and suffering, and habitually in the society of her elders, she early develops into a quaint, matter-of-fact little creature, such as might well disconcert a peacock like the Reverend Meekin.

To Frere, whose knowledge of other women has been mainly immoral, her innocence and wilfulness, and her instinctive dislike of him, serve as a strong attraction. Though he becomes her husband by means of a cruel fraud, he never fully gains her trust, and the estrangement so tragically sealed in the last chapter of the novel comes almost as a relief to the sympathetic reader of her sad history. Sylvia Vickers, despite the gloomy environment of her youth, is throughout an intensely womanly woman, the delicate conception of whose character surely places her creator far above the rank of the cynics in literature.

Not the least of the elements which combine to make *His Natural Life* one of the most remarkable novels of the century is the occasional skilful varying of its painful realism

with a colouring of romance, as in the relations between Dawes and Sylvia : his absorbing devotion when she is so strangely made
dependent upon him at the deserted settlement ; his long-continued confidence that she
will effect his vindication and deliverance ;
and, finally, the dominant motive of securing
her safety against North with which he
escapes from the gaol at Norfolk Island, and
joins her in the doomed schooner on its last
voyage to Van Diemen's Land.

What Oliver Wendell Holmes called ' the
Robinson Crusoe touches' in the story—
including the experiences of the marooned
party at Macquarie Harbour, and those of
Rex in his escape through the Devil's Blow-
hole --also help to leave with the reader of
the novel an ineffaceable memory.

HENRY KINGSLEY.

WHAT are the special qualities that constitute the permanent charm of Henry Kingsley's early novels? Some English critics, judging him by principles of literary art, have said that his best. work is in many places of slovenly construction, deficient in dramatic power, and imitative in expression. A series of episodes, they observe, supply the place of a plot in *The Recollections of Geoffry Hamlyn;* the central motive of *The Hill-yars and the Burtons* is an impossible story of a young woman's self-sacrifice ; and the Thackerayan mannerisms in *Ravenshoe* are an offensive blemish upon an otherwise fine novel.

As a set-off to these defects, which are of less real consequence than may appear from their brief enumeration, Kingsley has been freely credited with a certain ever-pleasing vivacity and gallantry of style far too rare in literature to be overlooked. The warmest of his admirers in his own country have even attempted to raise him to a position above that of his more celebrated brother.

The task of comparing Kingsley the poet, preacher, and reformer, with Kingsley the laughing, genial teller of stories who never cherished a hobby in his life, would seem to be as superfluous on general grounds as it is premature in respect of the only possible question as to which of them is likely to be best remembered a generation or two hence. Only in one particular does it seem quite safe to predict—namely, that whatever may be the future standing of one who is said to have never penned a story without a didactic purpose of some kind, Henry Kingsley is certain of a permanent place in the literature of the young country where he encountered both the best and the worst experiences of his life.

The English estimate of his novels—mainly

a technical one—having been recorded, it
seems to the present writer that something
of interest might be said of them from, as
far as possible, the Australian point of view,
the standpoint of the reader who knows the
country of Sam Buckley and Alice Brentwood, and has lived some of their life. Two
out of the three best novels are largely
Australian in matter, and the reasons for
their enduring popularity in the colonies are
among the best grounds of the favour in
which the author is held by the average
English reader, to leave out of reckoning
for the moment the literary expert. *Geoffry
Hamlyn* and *The Hillyars and the Burtons*
have obvious faults, but in most respects
they are the highest, because the least artificial, expression of Kingsley's powers. A
consideration of some of their more noticeable qualities will perhaps afford the clearest
answer to the question which opens this
essay.

Henry Kingsley was one of the many
impecunious young Englishmen of education
and adventurous spirit who sought fortune

on the gold-fields of Australia between 1851
and 1860, and were rewarded in some cases
with ready wealth, but in far more with bitter
disappointment.   Leaving Oxford without a
degree in the company of two fellow-students,
he hurried off to the Victorian gold-fields,
which were then in the early sensational
period of their development, and attracting
people from all parts of the world.   It was
the time when the ordinary business of the
colonies could scarcely be carried on at any
sacrifice—when some of the more perplexed
employers in the adjoining territory of New
South Wales had urged Governor Fitzroy to
proclaim martial law and peremptorily pro-
hibit mining, 'in order that the inducement
which seemed so irresistible to persons to
quit their ordinary occupations might be removed.'   In the country districts crops were
left unreaped and sheep unshorn; in the
towns masters did their own work or paid
excessively to have it half done; while the
harbours were filled with vessels whose crews
had deserted to join in the general scramble
for gold.   No one was content to stand

behind a counter all day and hear of nuggets being found up-country which sold for over four thousand pounds. 'As well attempt to stop the influx of the tide as stop the rush to the diggings,' was the reply given by Fitzroy to his petitioners.

Ex-military and naval officers, professional men, convicts from Van Diemen's Land, picturesque cut-throats from the Californian and Mexican mines, Chinese, and many other varieties of the human species, rubbed shoulders and lived generally in remarkable order and amity in the crowded canvas cities of Turon, Mount Alexander, Ballarat, and Bendigo. In 1852, the year before Kingsley's arrival, seventy thousand of them were toiling in Victoria alone.

Such were the times and the people which gave the future novelist his first practical experience of colonial life. The varied knowledge that he accumulated, first of the gold-fields and later of pastoral life and the towns, was the only reward of his five years' voluntary exile from England. During his absence he never wrote to his parents, and

they thought him dead.   His reticence as to
his unsuccessful struggles was continued
when he returned home, and not relaxed in
later life even to his wife.

An interesting memoir by Mr. Clement
Shorter, prefixed to a new edition of
Kingsley's novels, briefly describes his
school-days and literary career, but is almost
wholly silent concerning the eventful years
spent in the colonies.   There is a single
reference to the period which succeeded his
gold-digging days, when want forced him to
seek a less precarious occupation.   For a
time, it seems, he was a mounted policeman
in New South Wales, until, 'compelled by
duty to attend an execution, he was so much
affected that he threw up the appointment
in disgust.'   Then, like many another unlucky digger, he was obliged to travel the
country in search of work on the sheep and
cattle stations.

A well-known pastoralist of the western
district of Victoria, the late Hon. Philip
Russell, was accustomed to describe to his
friends the arrival at his station many years

ago of a party of ' sundowners ' (*i.e.*, tramps),
among whom was Kingsley, looking 'very
much down on his luck.' Soon found to be
no ordinary swagman, he was made a guest
at the station, where he remained for several
months. The most agreeable glimpse obtainable of his colonial life is given in *Old
Melbourne Memories*, a little collection of
sketches published by Rolf Boldrewood
twelve years ago.

At the period which they recall, Boldrewood was a young man, and making the
experiment in squatting which, though disastrous in its ultimate commercial results,
was afterwards turned to a rich literary
account by him. A friend of his named
Mitchell occupied a station in western
Victoria named Langa-willi, and there on
one occasion Boldrewood met Kingsley.
The passage in which he gracefully records
the event is worth quoting in full.

'Why Langa-willi,' he says, ' will always
be a point of interest in my memory, apart
from other reasons, for I spent many a
pleasant day there, was that Henry Kingsley

lived there the chief part of a year as a guest
of Mitchell's.

' It was at Langa - willi that *Geoffry
Hamlyn*, that immortal work, the best
Australian novel, and for long the only one,
was written. In the well-appointed sitting-
room of that most comfortable cottage one
can imagine the gifted but somewhat ill-
fated author sitting down comfortably after
breakfast to his " copy," when his host had
ridden forth with his overseer to make-believe
to inspect the flocks, but in reality to get an
appetite for lunch.

' I like to think of them both spending the
evening sociably in their own way, both
rather silent men—Kingsley writing away
till he had covered the regulation number of
sheets or finished the chapter, perhaps when
the bushrangers came to Garoopna ; Mitchell
reading steadily, or writing up his home
correspondence ; the old housekeeper coming
in with the glasses at ten o'clock ; then a
tumbler of toddy, a smoke on the verandah,
or over the fire if in winter, and so to bed.
Peaceful, happy, unexciting days and nights,

good for Mitchell, who was not strong, and
for his talented guest, who was not always
so profitably employed. I suspect that in
England, where both abode in later years,
they often looked back with regret to the
peerless climate, the calm days, the restful
evenings spent so far beyond the southern
main at Langa-willi.'

At least one of them must often have
recalled those days as being among the
happiest of a none too happy life. The
main features of Kingsley's career after he
returned to England may be summarised
here in a few words. The distinct success
as a novelist which he won during the first
four or five years was not maintained. His
work lessened in interest as he lost the *verve*
of youth, increased his leaning towards
romance, and became more conventional in
his methods.

He essayed journalism for a time, first as
editor of the Edinburgh *Daily Review*, and
later as a correspondent of the same journal
at the Franco-German War. As an editor
he was a failure, through being without the

necessary technical training, and it does not appear that he had much opportunity to distinguish himself as a war correspondent. The writing of fiction was his proper work, and his success at it seemed always to be in proportion to the amount of personal experience which he employed to support the superstructure of his somewhat reckless fancy. Those of Kingsley's friends who contribute to the brief memoir of his life bear unanimous testimony to the personal brightness and kindness of which he has left so worthy a memorial in his first novels.

It is characteristic of Kingsley that he never wrote an ungenerous word of the country which sent him away empty-handed from the store of its riches. Not even a suggestion of the fruitless toil and the disillusionment which he shared with scores of other amateur diggers during the first two years of his colonial life finds expression in any of his novels. His choice of incident and adventure in *Geoffry Hamlyn* seems to imply a deliberate ignoring of what was

by far the most striking development of
Antipodean life in the decade of 1850-60.

The gold-fields were then in a sense an
epitome of the world, the centre at which
all men's thoughts converged, an ever-
changing spectacle, a daily source of novelty
and suggestion.   The life of the squatters
was primitive, inferior in variety, and marked
only by a rapid accumulation of wealth, which
was in itself but a part of the general prosperity created by the discovery of gold.   If
Kingsley wished to repress memories which
it would have been against his cheerful
nature to perpetuate, he succeeded with
singular completeness.

Save the technical knowledge of geology
shown by Trevittick in *The Hillyars and
the Burtons*, and by the encyclopædic Dr.
Mulhaus in his lecture at the picnic in the
grass-covered crater of Mirngish, there is
nothing to suggest that the author had any
personal acquaintance with mining in the
colonies.   The experience that was so fresh
and abundant in his mind is put aside in
favour of a set of facts and pictures not even

incidentally connected with life on the gold-fields.

As if to emphasise the motive of his choice, if motive there was, he selected the pre-auriferous period for the Australian parts of his stories. His squatters become wealthy by a comparatively slow process, extending over some sixteen years. The squatters of the gold period would certainly seem better adapted to the purposes of fiction. There is, indeed, more than a suggestion of romance in the sudden burst of fortune which within the first few years after 1851 raised so many of them from positions of struggling uncertainty to affluence, with incomes varying from ten to twenty thousand pounds, and in some few cases as high as thirty thousand pounds, a year.

The first and last use Kingsley made of his gold-fields experience is seen in the sketch of mining of the successful sort in the third volume of *The Hillyars and the Burtons*, but this is so slight that it might have been imagined by a writer who had never handled a shovel or a washing-cradle in his life.

The Australian people have so often been
the subject of flippant and ill-natured criticisms, that they can readily appreciate any
liberal estimate of themselves in whatever
form it may be placed before their kindred in
Great Britain.   It is a fact, as natural as it is
undeniable, that they are very sensitive to
praise or blame.   What wounds them more
than adverse comment itself, is the circumstance of its often proceeding from persons
who have accepted without warning their too
prompt and trustful hospitality.

To anyone but the incorrigibly confident
and good-natured Antipodean, the lesson
would be obvious, namely, that the distinguished visitor should be petted less, and
left more dependent upon his own devices
in the collection of materials for the inevitable
book or magazine article.   Though the result
might be the same, there would be no in-
gratitude, and the critic would be less able
to pose as an impartial inside observer of
Australian society.

Perhaps, indeed, though this implies a
somewhat wild flight of imagination, he

might altogether escape the fatal sense of compulsion towards printers'-ink, under which the traveller of a few weeks' or months' experience commonly labours when once he has extricated himself from the blandishments of Toorak or Darling Point.

It is true that Australia has received many a compliment from casual writers, but to Australians themselves it is always a question whether these kindnesses are not outbalanced by the inaccuracies which surround them. For it may as well be said at once that the younger colonists do not relish being denied all native individuality, and depicted with a complaisant condescension as mere imitators of English life. It is well to be a Briton, they say, but better to be an Australian. And who shall say that their self-satisfaction is not healthy and pardonable?

By contrast with the judgments of persons to whom candour concerning the colonies seems to be a stern duty, Henry Kingsley's pictures of the pioneer life of Australia fifty years ago, and his liberal estimate (since largely realised) of the future of the country, find more enduring appreciation than would, perhaps, be accorded such writing in ordinary circumstances.

The good feeling that shines on every page of *Geoffry Hamlyn* would earn gratitude from Australian readers were the story not in itself spirited and absorbing. If from the personal experiences with which this first novel is crowded Kingsley excluded everything that might be unfavourable to the reputation of Australia and its people, he at least told nothing that was untrue. His record of the country is a generous one, but there is no flattery—at least, none of the grosser sort.

It is one of his supreme qualities, too, that while delighting to preserve unmodified the British spirit and traditions in his emigrant colonists, he surrounds their offspring with a subtle distinction. Some of the manly strength and courtly serenity, the truth, honour, and delicacy of the ideal Englishman and Englishwoman they reproduce ; and then there is added a something caught from the warm air and the broader expanses of the

South—a new impulse, a deeper tinge in the blood, a greater trust in human nature.

As befitting the early period of which the novelist wrote, this difference is not strongly marked, and is more readily recognisable in the light of colonial experience than without it ; but it clearly exists. Its continuation at the present day is far more apparent. Kingsley's young Australians are home-taught, and necessarily display most of the characteristics of their British parents. But, still, they show themselves types of a new race, which has now its hundreds of representatives in the homes of the Australian gentry.

Of such was the young squatter who so attracted the attention of Mr. Froude at the first station he visited in Victoria. 'He had till within a month or two been herding cattle in Queensland, doing the work for four years of the roughest emigrant field hand, yet had retained the manners of the finest of fine gentlemen—tall, spare-loined, agile as a deer, and with a face that might have belonged to Sir Lancelot.' Of course, the genial author of *Oceana* made no pretence of minute observation in the account of his travels. Had he not been content to fly through the country, viewing it mainly, as he admits, from 'softest sofas' of 'a superlative carriage lined with blue satin,' he might have seen not one, but many fine specimens of what Sir George Bowen has aptly called the working aristocracy of Australia.

The little Arcadian kingdom—cheerful, self-contained, and picturesque—of the Buckleys, the Brentwoods, and their historian, Geoffry Hamlyn, of the Mayfords, Tom Troubridge, Mary Hawker, and the rest, far from illustrates all the intermittent successes and hardships which have commonly attended squatting in Australia. The toil, loneliness, and monotony of the occupation are scarcely mentioned. The aspect represented is almost entirely the agreeable one.

There is, it must be admitted, some ground for the charge that he has made squatting life 'too much like a prolonged picnic.' Had Kingsley been himself a pastoralist, a hundred minute experiences might have obtained expression which he has avoided. In this respect the historical value of his work is less than it might have been. But the compensating gain in human interest more than justifies the author's choice of treatment. He never allowed himself to forget that he was telling a story, that he was writing the adventures of a small group of emigrant English families, not a history of colonial settlement and its difficulties. Nor does he ever take advantage of the fact that, with the exception of two or three others whose works are collections of sketches rather than novels, and whose names are now almost forgotten, he was the first to describe in fiction the rural life of the country, to recognise the beginning of an aristocracy of landholders, and to commemorate the pervading spirit of cheerful confidence to which so much of the rapid early development of Australia was due.

It may well be regretted that one who had so keen an eye for all that was best in the social life of the country, at one of its most interesting periods, should not have written a volume or two of reminiscences, but no colonial reader would wish *Geoffry Hamlyn*

or *The Hillyars and the Burtons* to have
been made the vehicle of more descriptive
matter than they contain. Kingsley was
more sparing in the use of local colour and
incident than Boldrewood and some of the
younger writers are, though in his first novel
a few passages occur which may be considered unnecessary, including the story told
by the hut-keeper to Hamlyn in the presence
of the disguised bushrangers, the whisking of
Captain Blockstrop and his friends on and off
the stage, and the story of the lost child. The
latter, however, like Dr. Mulhaus' geological
lecture, has the merit of being one of the best
pieces of prose the author ever wrote, and
gives Sam Buckley and Cecil Mayford an
opportunity for a dramatic settlement of the
order of their suit for the hand of Alice Brentwood. In the main narrative the periods of
'dull prosperity' are expressly avoided. After
that first beautiful picture of the pioneer
settlement, ' the scene so venerable, so
ancient, so seldom seen in the old world—
the patriarchs moving into the desert with all
their wealth to find a new pasture land '—

the action of the story is rapidly advanced to
the later days of their success. The estate
which has been the home of Major Buckley's
forefathers for generations no longer providing a competence, he has resolutely left it
for the land where he is to find 'a new heaven
and a new earth.' Unlike so many of the
pioneers, he has bade a final good-bye to
England, but that it is *not* 'for ever' one can
safely predict from the outset. He sees the
old country in long years after, when, with
some of the wealth garnered on the rolling
prairies of Northern Australia, his son has
proudly bought back the family domain of
Clere in all the completeness of its original
acres. Within a few brief chapters the
colonists are discovered in the security of
assured wealth. Sitting under their station
verandahs, they can contemplate almost with
calmness the death of their cattle by hundreds,
and the devastation of their runs by Bush
fires. They have arrived at the period when
'there was money in the bank, claret in the
cellar, and race-horses in the paddock.'
Meanwhile, the old Devonshire life is

becoming a dim memory. They have kept their promise to create a new Drumston in the wilderness, and are well content with their homes among the southern fern-clad hills. The history of their intercourse approaches the character of an epic. Over his structure of realism—of life as he saw it and lived it himself—the writer has cast a softening glow of romance, through which are seen the beauties of ideal friendship, of youthful love, family affection, pride of nationality, and charity towards all mankind.

Kingsley was a lover of his fellows, and wont to declare that the proportion of good to bad in human nature was as ten to one the world over. This tenet of his religion he infused in some measure into all his novels. It is this they teach if they teach anything. From it spring their most vital qualities. The best of the stories possess that 'certain intellectual and spiritual atmosphere,' which Matthew Arnold assigned as the gift of literary genius. Their virility and right feeling are unmistakable, and insensibly teach the practice of a silent and kindly forbearance towards the foibles of our fellow-creatures. The names alone of the principal characters in *Geoffry Hamlyn* recall scene after scene in their idyllic life to which it refreshes the mind to return. There is Major Buckley, a hero of Waterloo, gigantic in stature, refined, calmly courageous --a fitting leader of the settlement ; Mrs. Buckley, high-bred, stately, self-reliant, a model English matron ; Tom Troubridge, the big, merry Devonian, grown with prosperity weighty and didactic in his speech, and thinking of turning his attention to politics ; Miss Thornton, the dignified, sweet old maid, born to spend her life in uncomplaining service of others ; Mary Hawker, tragic, passionate, paying the slow penalty of youthful wilfulness ; Captain Brentwood, of Wellington's artillery, and his gallant son Jim, who is sighing for a red coat and a commission ; Sam and Alice, the young lovers so nearly lost to each other 'in the year when the bushrangers came down ' ; and Dr. Mulhaus, the mysterious German, with his good-humoured roar, first heard at

old Drumston, and with us to the end, who
is everybody's friend and counsellor, and
beloved by all—except George Hawker, of
whose 'tom-cat' skull he has made that
amusingly audacious examination at the
beginning of their acquaintance. It is delightful to find all the faces familiar in the old
land reappearing in the new, even though
the coincidences which attend their coming
seem too good to be true.

But the reader forgets the occasional loose-
jointedness of the story in contemplation of
the swift succession of happy scenes created
for him. In these there is nothing dubious
or artificial. They are sketches straight from
the life of the country, and it is their beauty
that makes *Geoffry Hamlyn* a classic in Australian literature.

Among the characters, there are so many
who inspire us with love rather than mere
interest, that a multiplicity of similar scenes,
of conversations, rides, pleasure-excursions,
and other intercourse, which in another book
might prove wearisome, becomes here the
best enjoyment of the reader. With what

vivacity and gusto the author describes the
visits exchanged between the home stations,
and the comforts and happiness which they
reveal! Half the book is made up of them,
and yet the majority remain sufficiently clear
in the memory to be recalled separately.
Brentwood, who is at first fifty miles away,
buys a station near at hand, he and Buckley
having become inseparable, and now Baroona,
Garoopna, and Toonarbin are only a few miles
apart. 'There was always a hostage from
one staying as a guest at the other.' The
visits were generally unannounced, and the
visitors stayed as long as they felt inclined
to. The effects of this custom are once
amusingly illustrated at the home of Captain
Brentwood. It is when the members of the
little colony hear of the arrival of his beautiful daughter from Sydney, where she has
been at school. 'That week one of those
runs upon the Captain's hospitality took place
which are common enough in the Bush, and,
although causing a temporary inconvenience,
are generally as much enjoyed by the enter-
tainers as the entertained. Everybody during

8

this next week came to see them, and nobody went back again. So by the end of the week there were a dozen or fourteen guests assembled, all uninvited, and apparently bent on making a long stay of it.' They help one another when there is work to be done, dine sumptuously, picnic luxuriously. Kingsley has properly made eating and drinking a noticeable part of the hearty full-bodied existence of his squatters and their friends.

There is no class of people who have a better capacity for enjoying the material comforts of life than the country gentlemen of Australia. Major Buckley is just the sort of person one might have expected to hold decided views on the subject of dining as an art. To dine in the middle of the day was, in his opinion, a gross abuse of the gifts of Providence. 'I eat my dinner not so much for the sake of the dinner itself as for the after-dinnerish feeling which follows—a feeling that you have nothing to do, and that, if you had, you'd be shot if you'd do it.'

On another occasion the author himself preaches a similarly agreeable doctrine, concluding with the advice : ' My brother, let us breakfast in Scotland, lunch in Australia, and dine in France, till our lives end.'

Nor is the kindred subject of lounging in midsummer forgotten. Anyone in an arm-chair under a broad Australian verandah, who fetched anything for himself, would, in the author's opinion, 'show himself a man of weak mind.' Niggers were all that a Southern gentleman wanted to complete his comfort when the sun was at baking-point. Mrs. Beecher Stowe's teachings undergo a playful deprecation. Did she know the exertion required for cutting up a pipe of tobacco in a hot north wind ; or the amount of perspiration and anger superinduced by knocking the head off a bottle of Bass in January ; or the physical prostration caused by breaking two lumps of hard white sugar in a pawnee before a thunderstorm ? The Southern gentleman undertakes to affirm that she didn't.

In the conversation of Kingsley's colonists,

the business of the squatter, his hopes, fears
and struggles, find no place, and the idea of
hard work is never obtruded for its own sake.
The talk is the talk of a cultured class who
live wholesome lives and have no cares. The
twelve thousand miles that separate them
from the centre of their intellectual life are
obliterated.   The men preserve their individual tastes, together with that comradeship
and mutual considerateness which have their
origin in the best traditions of college life.
The same loyalty and chivalry are prominently reproduced in the characters of *Ravenshoe* and *Silcote of Silcotes.*   But in *Geoffry
Hamlyn* these qualities are perhaps more
noticeable (at all events to a colonial reader)
than in the later novels, because of the
contrast they furnish to the essentially com-
petitive life of modern Australia.   Brentwood
is ' excessively attached to mathematics, and
has leisure to gratify his hobby '; Harding,
'an Oxford man,' is 'an inveterate writer of
songs,' a pastime which only the annual
business of shearing is permitted to interrupt;
Buckley is intent on the education of his son,

in which he is careful to provide for a knowledge of the Latin Grammar; while Doctor
Mulhaus finds the new country an even
better field than the old one for his researches
as a naturalist and geologist. In telling his
story, Kingsley seems, in short, to have
treated pioneer squatting in Australia as the
brighter aspects of English country life have
been treated in fiction for generations past.
He expends his best efforts in showing the
picturesque surroundings and interior comfort
of Australian homes. Neither their tables
nor their bookshelves lack any of the best
luxuries of the hour. The greyness and
rawness of their environment are not touched
upon. Marcus Clarke could never have
shown the Australian people so much of the
beauty of their strange fauna and flora as
can be found in *Geoffry Hamlyn*. He would
have allowed the budding civilisation of the
country to be swallowed up in sombre
desolate forests, or appear as lonely specks
on bleached and thirsty plains. Though he
might intend the contrary, that, substantially,
would be the final impression left on the

mind of the reader. Australian scenery
awed and depressed him. With all his
powers of graphic expression, he could
seldom write of it without exaggeration. It
was the fascination of the grotesque rather
than the picturesque that he felt. Kingsley,
though scarcely so graceful and vivid a
describer, had a keener and more constant
sense of natural beauty. His vision was
unclouded by the peculiar susceptibility of
temperament which narrowed the view of
his brilliant contemporary. He could not
have indulged in rhetorical flourishes at
the expense of accuracy, as in the familiar
passage professing to give the Australian
view of 'our trees without shade, our flowers
without perfume, our birds who cannot fly,
our beasts who have not yet learned to walk
on all fours.' A comparison of Marcus
Clarke's too often quoted description with
the sketches of landscape given in, say,
the twentieth, twenty-eighth and thirty-sixth
chapters of *Geoffry Hamlyn* and at the beginning of the third volume of *The Hillyars
and the Burtons* curiously illustrates how

far the appreciation of Australian scenery
depends upon the point of view of the
observer.

Kingsley's descriptions, like all else that
he wrote of the country, breathe an unmistakable personal enjoyment. They are the
natural expression of a happy disposition,
just as is the boyish fun with which he
surrounds the love-making of his characters.
' Halbert kicked Jim's shins under the table,
and whispered : " You've lost your money,
old fellow !"' when Sam Buckley, flushed
and happy, rejoined his friends in the sitting-
room at Garoopna, after proposing to Alice in
the garden. Jim Brentwood had peevishly
bet his friend that the lovers would go on
shilly-shallying half their lives ; but Halbert,
with keener vision, had foreseen the very
hour of their betrothal, and made a bet of
five pounds on the event. More comical
still is the spectacle of Hamlyn ducking
under the bedclothes to escape the boot that
is about to be flung at him, for laughingly
discrediting the story of which his bosom-
friend Stockbridge has tragically unburdened

himself concerning the evaporation of his love for Mary Hawker.

Whether in recording the actions and dialogue of his characters, or in describing scenery and the habits of the birds and animals which figure so often in his first novel, Kingsley always reflected some of his own happiness. It is not wit nor subtle humour, but a combination of pure mirth with the enthusiasm of warm friendship, that maintains one's interest in the simple life of the new Drumston. There is an abundance of farcical fun and playfulness which force laughter, and never approach an unkindness. The men avoid being smart at each other's expense; and if they cannot claim to be clever or heroic, they are at least good fellows, any one of whom might serve as a model of manliness.

Kingsley's knowledge of household pets was of the kind exhibited by persons who have spent some period of their lives in loneliness, with only the companionship of dumb creatures. He was an acute observer of their peculiarities, with the noting of

which he combined a whimsical exaggeration. The account of the menagerie which
Sam Buckley found at Garoopna on the
occasion of his memorable first meeting with
Alice Brentwood is almost unique in Australian literature.

Buckley's ride to rescue his sweetheart
from the bushrangers is one of the most
moving and dramatic incidents in the book,
and a good specimen of Kingsley's graphic
narrative style. A band of the outlaws who
were the terror of pioneer colonists fifty
years ago have risen in the district, and, after
committing outrages at one station, are reported to be riding on to another twenty
miles distant. At the latter, Captain Brentwood's home, Alice happens to be alone.
When the terrible news comes to her young
lover, he is at Baroona, which by the shortest
road is ten miles from Brentwood's. What
start have the bushrangers had, and will they
arrive before him?

Sam's noble horse, Widderin, a horse with a pedigree
a hundred years old, stood in the stable. The buying
of that horse had been Sam's only extravagance, for

which he had often reproached himself, and now this day he would see whether he would get his money's-worth out of that horse or no.

I followed him up to the stable, and found him putting the bridle on Widderin's beautiful little head. Neither of us spoke; only when I handed him the saddle, and helped him with the girths, he said, 'God bless you!'

I ran out and got down the slip-rails for him. As he rode by, he said, 'Good-bye, Uncle Jeff; perhaps you won't see me again'; and I cried out, 'Remember your God and your mother, Sam, and don't do anything foolish.' Then he was gone. . . .

Looking across the plains the way he should go, I saw another horseman toiling far away, and recognised Doctor Mulhaus. Good Doctor! he had seen the danger in a moment, and by his ready wit had got a start of everyone else by ten minutes. The Doctor, on his handsome, long-bodied Arabian mare, was making good work of it across the plains, when he heard the rush of a horse's feet behind him, and turning, he saw tall Widderin bestridden by Sam, springing over the turf, gaining on him stride after stride. In a few minutes they were alongside of one another.

'Good lad!' cried the Doctor. 'On, forwards; catch her, and away to the woods with her! Bloodhound Desborough will be on their trail in half an hour. Save her, and we will have noble vengeance!'

Sam only waved his hand in good-bye, and sped on across the plain like a solitary ship at sea. The good horse, with elastic and easy motion, fled on his course like a bird, lifting his feet clearly and rapidly through the grass. The brisk south wind filled his wide nostrils as he turned his graceful neck from side to side, till. finding that work was meant, and not play, he began to hold his head straight before him, and rush steadily forward. . . .

One stumble now, and it were better to lie down on the plain and die. He was in the hands of God, and he felt it. He said one short prayer, but that towards the end was interrupted by the wild current of his thoughts. Was there any hope? They, the devils, would have been drinking at the Mayfords', and perhaps would go slow ; or would they ride fast and wild ? After thinking a short time, he feared the latter. They had tasted blood, and knew that the country would be roused on them shortly. . . .

Here are a brace of good pistols, and they with care shall give account, if need be, of two men. After that. nothing. It were better—so much better—not to live if one were only ten minutes too late. . . . Now he was in the forest again, and now as he rode quickly down the steep sandy road among the bracken, he heard the hoarse rush of the river in his ears, and knew the end was well-nigh come. . . . Now the house was in sight, and now he cried aloud some wild inarticulate sound of thankfulness and joy. All was as peaceful as ever, and Alice, unconscious, stood white-robed in the verandah. feeding her birds.

As he rode up he shouted to her and beckoned. She came running through the house, and met him breathless at the doorway.

'The bushrangers, Alice, my love !' he said. 'We must fly this instant ; they are close to us now.'

She had been prepared for this. She knew her duty

well, for her father had often told her what to do No
tears! no hysterics! She took Sam's hand without a
word, and, placing her fairy foot upon his boot, vaulted
up into the saddle before him. . . . They crossed the
river, and dismounting, they led the tired horse up the
steep slope of turf that surrounded a little castellated tor
of bluestone. . . .

'I do not see them anywhere, Alice,' said Sam
presently. 'I see no one coming across the plains.
They must be either very near us in the hollow of the
river-valley, or else a long way off.'

''There they are!' said Alice. 'Surely there is a large
party of horsemen on the plain, but they are seven or
eight miles off.'

'Ay, ten,' said Sam. 'I am not sure that they are
horsemen.' Then he said suddenly in a whisper, 'Lie
down, my love, in God's name! Here they are, close
to us!'

There burst on his ear a confused round of talking
and laughing, and out of one of the rocky gullies leading
towards the river came the men they had been flying
from, in number about fourteen. They had crossed the
river, for some unknown reason, and to the fear-struck
hiders it seemed as though they were making straight
towards their lair.

He had got Widderin's head in his breast, blindfolding
him with his coat, for should he neigh now they were
undone indeed! As the bushrangers approached, the
horse began to get uneasy and paw the ground, putting
Sam in such an agony of terror that the sweat rolled
down his face. In the midst of this he felt a hand on
his arm, and Alice's voice, which he scarcely recognised,

said in a fierce whisper: 'Give me one of your pistols,
sir !'

'Leave that to me !' he replied, in the same tone.

'As you please,' she said; 'but I must not fall alive
into their hands. Never look your mother in the face
again if I do.'

He gave one more glance around, and saw that the
enemy would come within a hundred yards of their
hiding-place. Then he held the horse faster than ever
and shut his eyes.

Was it a minute only, or an hour, until they heard
the sound of the voices dying away in the roar of the
river, and, opening their eyes once more, looked into
one another's faces ? Faces they thought that they had
never seen before—so each told the other afterwards—
so wild, so haggard, and so strange.

If, as Professor Masson says, 'it is by his
characters that a novelist is chiefly judged,'
Henry Kingsley's future reputation will be
found to depend almost solely on what
he accomplished in *Geoffry Hamlyn*, *The
Hillyars and the Burtons* and *Ravenshoe*.
In the first two of these there is an abundance of original observation and little conscious study of character. The vivid
Australian scenes of the one, and the Chelsea
life of the other, are transcripts of the
author's own memories. His knowledge of

the squatters he got by working for them and living with them ; what he knew of police and convicts and bushrangers he learned in doing police duty ; the life of the Burtons, as told in ' Jim Burton's Story,' was that which the author saw during his boyhood round his father's old rectory on Chelsea Embankment.

' He seemed to me,' says Mrs. Thackeray Ritchie, ' to have lived his own books, battled them out and forced them into their living shapes, to have felt them and been them all.' Hardly all—one feels bound to say. The remark is entirely true of nearly everything in *Geoffry Hamlyn* and of three-fourths of *The Hillyars and the Burtons*, but to *Ravenshoe* it applies in a more limited degree, and to some of the later novels scarcely ever. Either through carelessness (of which one often suspects him) or deficiency of judgment, Kingsley more than once allowed the exigencies of his plots to destroy all consistency in his characters.

Thus, Squire Silcote, the clever old ex-lawyer, is made to retire from the world and brood for many years, and on quite in-

sufficient grounds, in the belief that his first
wife had been unfaithful, and had tried
to poison him. Nothing short of a condition of semi-insanity could explain his
conduct. In other respects the character
is finely conceived. Emma Burton, too, is a
perfectly natural and charming person until
she is employed to revive the old problem of
how far a sense of duty can triumph over the
power of love. Her devotion to her de-
formed brother is wrong, because it is unnecessary. But even if this were not the
case, it would be irrational in a woman so
eminently sensible and unromantic as she
is shown to be in the first half of the story.
Almost at the beginning of her voluntary
service she is represented as realising 'the
hideous fate to which she has condemned
herself in her fanaticism.' It is quite impossible to make the reader believe that,
loving Erne Hillyar as she did, she could for
years persist in rejecting him, and that her
brother would permit so much sacrifice on
his account.

The beautiful, crazy Gerty Neville is

another instance of perversion. Her silliness is exaggerated in order that she shall weary and disgust the *blasé* aristocrat who has married her. Some of her chatter is more inconceivable than the ' coo-ee-ing ' which Mr. Hornung's ' Bride from the Bush ' employed to attract the attention of a colonial acquaintance of hers in Rotten Row.

But the distortion which the character of Emma Burton undergoes, and the caricature of Gerty Neville, are, after all, easily pardonable faults in a story rich in noble thought and sympathy, bright with pretty, audacious nonsense, and containing such real personages as Jim Burton and his father and mother, Erne Hillyar, and the Honourable Jack Dawson.

Even in *Silcote of Silcotes* there are intermittent glimpses of finely-conceived character which almost outbalance the eccentricities of the Dark Squire and his sister, the fantastic meddler in foreign intrigue. Kingsley's skill lay chiefly in his portrayal of men, especially of young men, such as the dashing Charles Ravenshoe and his philosophic friend Marston (a study of the George

Warrington type); Lord Welter, Lieutenant
Hillyar, and Colonel Tom Silcote, reckless
profligates, but likeable fellows all; Frank
Maberly, the athletic curate; and Sam
Buckley, the type of an Australian country
gentleman. With old men he was less successful. Lord Saltire, the placid good-
natured cynic of *Ravenshoe*, is, however,
a clever exception. 'All old women are
beautiful,' says Kingsley in one of his stories,
and he never portrayed one that was not.
His best are Miss Thornton and Lady Ascot.
The younger women, excepting Mary Hawker
and Adelaide Summers, are rather slightly
drawn. Even Alice Brentwood is a somewhat indistinct personage compared with the
Australian girls of Mrs. Campbell Praed and
Ada Cambridge.

The superior position usually accorded
to *Ravenshoe* among Kingsley's novels is
merited more by the soundness of its plot
than by the naturalness of its characters. It
was the author's first essay in pure romance,
and, with Henry Kingsley, to build character
from imagination was always largely, some-

9

times extravagantly, to idealise. He loved
to people old country houses with walking
mysteries, to unravel tangled genealogies,
and discover secrets of youthful folly, to
apportion property to rightful heirs, and
endow his characters with a superhuman
generosity. When Charles Ravenshoe is
recovering from the long illness which ter-
minates the full series of his misfortunes, he
sends for Welter, the man who might be
considered his arch-enemy, who not so long
before that had seduced Charles's sister and
stole his *fiancée*. Ravenshoe is represented
as forgetting all his newly-suffered wrongs,
and thinking only of Welter as his favourite
schoolfellow and youthful companion. Anticipating doubts as to the feasibility of this,
the author proceeds to discuss the point with
the reader, as he does in many similar instances throughout the story. He appears
to have a constant anxiety about the impression he is making, and his comments and
confidences certainly become distasteful. But
this foible goes only a small way to discount
the sterling merits of the novel.

ADA CAMBRIDGE.

TOWARDS the close of 1890 the Australian booksellers—a cautious, conservative class in their attitude towards new fiction, especially that produced by the adventurous female writer of these latter days—began to display so marked an interest in the work of Ada Cambridge, that one not acquainted with the circumstances of the case might have credited them with a friendly—possibly a patriotic—desire to give due place to a newly-risen native genius. And when, in the following year, another story from the same pen appeared, the popularity of the author was firmly established.

The neat red volumes were on every stall; the Mudie of Melbourne gave them a place of honour in his show-window, and the leading critical review said that the second story possessed a charm which ought to induce even the person who ignored fiction on principle to make an exception in its favour. It was the kind of gratifying recognition that the public always believes itself eager to offer the deserving young writer. Yet Ada Cambridge's literary work had extended over no less a period than fifteen years. Of course, much of this delay in securing recognition might have been avoided. Probably in England she could have won a substantial reputation in a third of the time, and with half the labour expended by her in contributing to the Australian press. But, as the wife of a country clergyman, she had other matters besides literature to occupy her attention, and was content to write when there happened to be leisure for it, and to see her work in a few of the leading colonial newspapers.

About half a dozen novels were issued in this way, besides occasional articles and poems. The publication of the longer stories in the *Australasian*, a high-class weekly journal, ought in itself to have made a name for the author, and possibly would have done so, were they not in most cases so obviously a local product, and therefore not to be seriously considered. It was a repetition of the experience of Rolf Boldrewood. In the end, as usual, it was the English public that first accepted her novels for what they were worth.

Ada Cambridge is a native of Norfolk, the lonely fens and quaint villages of which are a picturesque background of some of her best stories. In 1870, shortly after her marriage, she went with her husband, the Rev. George Frederick Cross, a clergyman of the Church of England, to Wangaratta, in Victoria. After residing successively in several other country towns of this colony, they settled in 1893 at Williamstown, a waterside suburb of Melbourne.

A novel entitled *Up the Murray*, dealing with life in the colonies, was published by Ada Cambridge (the author continues to issue her work under her maiden name) in the Melbourne press in 1875. Others of the same character followed at irregular intervals. Two were issued in book-form by a London firm of publishers, but did not attain to much more than a library circulation.

When the author again came before the English public, it was with a novel in which the purely Australian interest was rigidly subordinated to dramatic quality and a richly sympathetic study of character. *A Marked Man* is the story of a younger son of an old English county family who, while sharing the pride and indomitable spirit of his ancestry, develops a hatred for conventional prejudices and religious cant, and, after making a final assertion of independence by marrying a farmer's daughter, emigrates to New South Wales to establish a name and fortune on his own account.

The first half of the action takes place in England, the remainder in the colonies. The natural beauties surrounding the home of the Delavels at Sydney are not less delicately and poetically described than the village life they have left behind in the mother country —the patriarchal rule of an old-fashioned,

rather pompous house, over a people retaining the hereditary respect of vassals for
their feudal lord; but the view given of
Australian society is, in keeping with the
relation to it of Richard Delavel and his
household, of the slightest kind.

Delavel and the only daughter whom he
has trained to be his second self, whose
comradeship makes him almost forget the
long-drawn thraldom of his early *mésalliance*,
live in a world so much and so necessarily
their own, that one is grateful for the good
taste which excluded from it the bustle and
commoner interests of colonial life. The
novel met with general, and in several instances cordial, favour in England, and since
then the author has yearly increased her
reputation.

Three out of five of the later novels are,
like *A Marked Man*, made comparatively
independent of the distinctively local interest
to which we have been accustomed in the
works of most Australian authors. It is not
possible, for example, to point out anything
in the shape of an essentially local first cause

for any of the principal incidents of *Not All
in Vain* and *A Marriage Ceremony.* The
passionate half-brute, Neil Hammond, who
pursues the heroine of the former story
across the world, and terrorises her with his
unwelcome attentions, would have met a
violent death, or himself have murdered
someone, in his own country or elsewhere
as inevitably as in Australia ; and the man
who killed him would not have found
Katherine Knowles less faithful during the
long years of his imprisonment had her sacrifice been under the daily observation of
Hammond's family and her own strait-laced
aunts in their East Norfolk home.

In *A Marriage Ceremony*, the only advantage secured by taking the story from
London to Melbourne—instead of to New
York, let us say—seems to lie in whatever
added strength the sense of greater distance
imparts to the temporary appearance of a
final separation between Betty Ochiltree and
her strangely-wedded husband. The marriage that was a condition of their inherit-
ance having been performed, bride and

bridegroom part in accordance with a previous agreement. The former reappears as a prominent figure in the society of modern Melbourne—the Melbourne of 1893, when the failure of banks and land companies was a regular subject of morning news.

Here, it might be supposed, was an opportunity for one or two vivid and instructive sketches of the sensational period that witnessed the proof of so much folly and its punishment, and wrought so many more effects on all classes of Australian society than could be noted in the common records of the time. But the great crisis is almost ignored in the novel. There are merely a few passing references to its progress, and a mention of the loss on the part of Mrs. Ochiltree of some of the wealth which she is beginning to regard as having been rather spuriously acquired.

Even the very successful story of the *Three Miss Kings* and *A Mere Chance* tell little of the city life of Australia, though their action is placed in it almost exclusively. The latter is a tale of match-making intrigue and money-worship in Toorak, but the main interest of the plot apart, the account of fashionable Melbourne is a singularly colourless one. As for Mrs. Duff-Scott and her Major, the amiable pair who in the character of leaders of Melbourne society undertake to find husbands for Elizabeth King and her sisters, and whose benevolent intentions are so effectually forestalled, they are as conventionally English as though they belonged to the pages of Miss Braddon or Mrs. Henry Wood.

Again, though during half of *Fidelis* we are given occasional impressive and delightful glimpses of Nature under southern skies, the principal characters are English, and in England is centred first and last the dominant pathos of the story. A complete absence of dialect from the novels helps to emphasise the author's slender use of extraneous aids to interest.

The influence of Ada Cambridge's twenty-five years' Australian experience is shown in her general outlook upon life, rather than in the details of her work. The prevailing tone of

her books is one of marked cheerfulness,
sincerity, and simplicity; she has a hearty
dislike for conventional stupidities, especially
for the mock-modesty that stifles honest
sentiment; and she gives emphatic endorse-
ment to the pleasant dictum (which seems so
much more feasible in sunny Australia than
in colder northern lands) that the second half
of life is not less fruitful and satisfying than
the first.

As the general effect of Ada Cambridge's
teaching, so far as it can be gathered from
her plots, and the few instances in which she
has permitted herself anything in the shape
of didactic expression, is to make us more
patient with life's complexities and perceptive
of its compensations, and more content with
whatever happiness may be drawn in our
way by the chain of accidents called Destiny,
so do her principal characters, in their foibles
and their strength—in the little acts and
impulses which qualify alike their heroism
and their baseness—tend to make us more
discriminative and charitable.

In almost every case they are strong

studies from some point of view. Of deliberate analysis there is very little ; but there are numerous realistic touches not commonly admitted in fiction, which, handled with skill and insight, keep the character within the pale of common experience and increase rather than alienate the reader's sympathy. Thus, Richard Delavel's outburst of relief upon the death of his first wife, so far from being vulgar and brutal, as it might have seemed in other circumstances, recalls and emphasises the high sense of duty and honour and the iron self-restraint which had enabled him to be in all essentials a good husband for twenty-five years to a cold-hearted creature, between whom and himself there had never been either common interest or feeling, and for whose sake he had relinquished the woman that would have been his real mate in intellect and sympathy. Delavel's housekeeper, who is also a privileged friend, takes him to task for his unseemly hurry to go in search of this old love before his wife had been a week in her grave. He makes no secret of his relief. ' The sense that I am free is turning my brain with joy,' he confesses.

'I say it because I feel it. I am aware that it is in very bad taste, but that doesn't make it the less true. Do you suppose people are never glad when their relations die? They are—very often; they can't help it; only they pretend they are not, because it seems so shocking. I don't pretend—at least, I need not pretend to you. The fault is not always—not all—on the side of the survivors, Hannah. I don't think I am any worse than those who pretend a grief that they don't feel. I was never unkind to her—never in my life, that I can remember. I did not kill her; I would have kept her alive as long as I possibly could. I think—I hope— that if I could have saved her by the sacrifice of my own life, I should have done it without a single moment's hesitation.'

' I am sure you would,' said Hannah.

' But,' he continued, with that unwonted fire blazing in his eyes, 'since dead she is, I *am* glad—I am, I am ! I am glad as a man who has been kept in prison is to be let out. It is not my fault; I would be sorry if I could. Some day, Hannah—some day, when we have been dust for a few hundred years—perhaps for a few score only— people will wake up to see how stupid it is to drive a man to be glad when his wife is dead. They are finding out so many things; they will find that out too in time.'

Probably it will still appear to many that Delavel's admission was at least indelicate and inconsistent with his chivalrous nature. It is not here possible to convey an adequate impression of his fiery spirit, his long heart-hunger, and the magnitude of the loss which a wholly uncongenial marriage must ever mean to such a man. When the full story of his life and that of his quietly 'implacable' wife is read, his conduct seems natural and excusable. It is as much a part of himself as the tremulous tenderness with which he ministers to the comfort of the frail Constance Bethune, after finding and bringing her home, or as his fierce grief when she dies.

Another very human spectacle that illustrates the author's method is the reunion of Betty and Rutherford Ochiltree—the frank selfishness of their mutual joy while the poor woman who had been an unconscious barrier between them lies dead under their roof. It is a somewhat painful episode, and precludes anything like high esteem for Rutherford, but it has the quality of intense actuality.

In like manner is Adam Drewe shorn of some of the merit of his devotion to the heroine of *Fidelis* by being shown in successive attachments to other women during his long exile in Australia. The author recognises that, 'the laws of literary romance being so much at variance with the laws of Nature,' Adam is certain to suffer in the reader's good opinion for having 'continued to hunger for feminine sympathy as well as his daily dinner.' No doubt his stature as a hero lessens when it appears that though the absent Fidelia was ever in his thoughts, and a daily source of inspiration to him as a writer, he twice narrowly escaped marriage— first with a servant girl at his lodgings, and afterwards with the daughter of his landlady —and that at another period of his colonial life he became involved in a disreputable kind of Bohemianism. But he is not disgraced by these lapses to the extent that the author anticipates; at all events, they make him more human than he could otherwise have been.

It is this power of infusing a robust humanity into her characters that makes the distinctive feature of Ada Cambridge's best novels. In each, whatever the quality of the

plot, there are always two or three personages
who talk and act as real men and women
do—now rationally or in obedience to custom,
now passionately or with that perversity
which, as the author once describes it, 'is
like a natural law, independent of other laws,
the only one that persistently defies our cal-
culations.' They are mostly big people with
big appetites. The beauty of the women is
the beauty of mind and of sound physical
health.

Susy Delavel was tall, well grown, straight
and graceful, with an intelligent, eager face,
though 'her mouth was large, her nose not
all it should have been, and her complexion
showed the want of parasols and veils.' She
was 'not handsome at all, but decidedly
attractive.'

Sarah French, the girl in *Fidelis* whose
comeliness so nearly drew the hero from his
old allegiance, has 'a strong and good, rather
than a pretty, face,' with a 'large and substantial figure.' Adam Drewe concluded on
first sight of her that she was a nice woman.
Later on he finds her 'looking the very in-

carnation of home, with her cheerful healthy face, her strong busy hands, her neat hair, her neat dress. . . . She might have sat for a statue of Motherhood—of Charity with a babe at her ample breast, and others clinging to her supporting hand ; Nature had so evidently intended her to play the part.'

Katherine Knowles has fine physical symmetry and a strong, frank face. While lacking 'the airs and graces, the superficial brightness, of conventional girlhood,' she is 'singularly vivid in her more substantial way.'

Betty Ochiltree's beauty, too, is of the kind that wears well. She has a face 'frank and spirited, firm of mouth and chin, kind and sweet, as honest as the day,' surmounting an ample body, and she carries herself with dignity, 'as few Australian girls can do.' And how impressive and consistent with her character is the noble, placid figure of Elizabeth King, 'perfect in proportion, fine in texture, full of natural dignity and ease!'

The author is fond of showing the attractiveness of such women at the age of thirty,

or even more. 'In real life,' she once
observes, 'the supremely interesting woman
is not a girl of eighteen, as she is in fiction.
Every man worth calling a man knows that.
A girl of that age . . . knows as much about
love as does a young animal in the spring,
and not a bit more. And the human male of
these days—so highly developed, so subtly
compounded - has grown out of the stage
when that much would satisfy him. I mean,
of course, the human male who in real life
answers to the hero in fiction—a man who
must have left, not only his teens, but his
twenties behind him.'

When one comes to the heroes, it is easy
to recall half a dozen commanding figures
who blunder in the most natural and amiable
manner in their affairs; who think a good
deal more of their immediate personal comforts than of religious or ethical abstractions;
who like their own way and try to get it;
who, in short, are mostly what the author
wishes them to appear—'the men out of
books that we meet every day.' Of little
men, in the physical sense, there are only

two of any importance, but even these are virile and masterful. A general aim of the stories would seem to be to show the sexes what each chiefly admires in the other. It is first a sort of apotheosis of the *mens sana in corpore sano*, and after that an illustration of the independent attractions of sympathy, gentleness, culture, and high character.

Though in most cases the strongest attachments are formed between men and women arrived at an age to discriminate beyond mere physical charm, nevertheless physical charm is the most powerful, though not always acknowledged, motive of their choice. 'Because of this,' says the pathetic Hilda Donne in *A Marriage Ceremony*, touching her cheek, which is terribly disfigured by a birth-mark, 'I have never had *love*. Can you think what that means? You can't. Once I thought I was not going to be quite shut out—once ; but I was mistaken. I have found out that it is for one's body that one is loved, and not for one's soul.'

Hilda unconsciously exaggerates, for it appears that Rutherford Hope, though at

first affected with disgust by her disfigure-
ment, and convinced that no healthy man
could consort with 'so unnatural a woman,'
had come at last to regard her as a possible
wife—before he was confronted with the
sudden temptation to secure a fortune by
wedding Betty Ochiltree, in compliance with
the conditions of her millionaire uncle's will.
Yet Hilda's comment is substantially sound.
Even Rutherford, with all the sense of his
mature years, and all the culture that enabled
him to appreciate her poetic gift, would
have had to argue himself into a marriage
with her.

The ugliness of Adam Drewe, from which
his mother turned in disgust at his birth,
and which in youth drove him across the
seas in an agony of sensitiveness from the
woman he loved, was a less serious affliction
than that of Hilda Donne ; but we know that
he continued to be keenly reminded of its
disadvantages long after time had proved
the sterling qualities of his manhood, lessened
his deformity, and brought him fame and
wealth.

Compared with the previous illustration, however, his case is at fault in failing to give a sufficient description of his deformity. But that he himself long thought it an insuperable bar to his happiness is clear. When he fell in love with Fidelia Plunket, she was temporarily blind. His affection for her was returned, and he knew it, but dreading the disillusionment that would ensue when her sight was restored, he fled to Australia and determined to abandon all thought of her as a wife. Urged to return, because 'when a woman *is* a woman,' and really in love with a man, 'there's no camel she won't swallow for him,' Drewe replied that his camel was just the one camel that no woman had been known to swallow, or, at any rate, to digest. And he remained—for twenty years.

The plots of Ada Cambridge's novels are of the episodical order, and the author, despite her openly-expressed scorn for the unnaturalness of the average conventional novel, has not disdained employment of some of its time-honoured methods. Occasionally she is at pains to explain the feasibility of coincidences employed to secure dramatic interest. They are certainly never of an impossible kind, and no one would deny the truism that real life abounds in them. But has not a distinguished writer aptly pointed out that there are matters in which fiction cannot compete with life ? As a rule, however, where a few such weaknesses exist, they do not count for much with the average reader when the principal scenes are as finely drawn as those in *A Marked Man* or *Fidelis*, or *The Three Miss Kings*. The latter story in some details puts a greater strain upon the credulity than any of the other novels, yet so well conceived and absolutely natural are the characters of the three girls, and so humorously and pictorially presented the chief incidents in their development, that the dubious points of the plot become almost insignificant. The qualities of the novel as a whole are similar to those which obscure the artistic defects of *Geoffry Hamlyn*, and which for thirty-seven years have made it one of the most popular of Australian stories.

In the presentation of tragic or pathetic
incidents lies Ada Cambridge's chief power,
as far as her plots are concerned. In *A
Marked Man* it is accompanied by her
highest achievements in portraying a variety
of well-contrasted character. *Fidelis*, which
opens at the Norfolk village of the earlier
novel, and reintroduces the Delavels, contains
fewer developed characters, as may also be
said of *A Marriage Ceremony*. But the
three novels are equal in the high standard
of their emotional quality. No quotation of
moderate size could do justice to any of the
principal scenes of *A Marked Man :* the
chivalrous sacrifice of Richard Delavel's
youthful marriage ; the inward repentance
of it for twenty-two years ; the revival of his
love for Constance Bethune ; his painful
anxiety for her health, hungry enjoyment of
her companionship, and anguish at her death ;
and his own death soon afterwards. In the
more briefly detailed tragedy that brings into
such striking relief the sprightly drama of
A Marriage Ceremony, there is a scene
giving a fair example of the author's style in

touching passages. When Hilda, deeply in love with Rutherford Hope, hears of his union with another woman, she takes the readiest means of effacing herself by suddenly marrying a shallow coxcomb who seeks her for mercenary reasons, and going with him to Australia. Years afterwards she is so affected by the sudden reappearance of Rutherford, and by subsequent ill-treatment received from her jealous husband, that an exhausting illness follows, and to save herself from insanity she commits suicide. Meanwhile the long separation of Rutherford and Betty Ochiltree, which began on the day of their marriage, is coming to an end, and Hilda's death removes the final impediment. Together they pay a last visit to the dead woman :

Incapable of speech, he lifted a tress of hair—flowing free over the rigid arms, because it was really pretty, and thus had to be made the most of—and pressed it a moment to his bearded mouth. In that gesture he seemed to ask her forgiveness for having been a man like other men, as Nature made them.

'Kiss *her*,' Betty whispered, pushing him a little. She, too, felt that it would be something, if not much,

to put to the account that was so frightfully ill-balanced
—a kiss from Rutherford before all was wholly over.

He stooped and laid his lips—scarcely laid them—on
the waxen forehead. And he thought how he had nearly
kissed her once, in the scented spring dusk, at her
father's gate, and been repelled at the last moment by
the thought of something that he could not see. . . .
He turned back the sheet and straightened it, and
nobody but hired undertakers had anything more to do
with Hilda Donne. He put out the lamps, leaving her
in the dark, which, as a living, nervous woman, she had
always been afraid of; and he took Betty in his arms to
comfort her a little, before he opened the door upon the
light and life of their own transfigured world.

There is a characteristic vein of realism
in the subsequent view of the lovers' self-
absorption and short-lived sorrow, and the
callousness of Donne.

No later than the same Saturday afternoon [Hilda was
buried in the morning], her Edward was cheering himself with his preparations for New Zealand, whither he
was easily persuaded to set off at once as a means of
distracting his mind from his domestic woes, and of
retiring gracefully from a Civil Service that was otherwise certain to dismiss him; and there he shortly found
a number of absorbing interests, including—as Rutherford had predicted—a rosy-cheeked second wife, who, as
he wrote to Mrs. Ochiltree when announcing his engagement, was all that heart could wish, and had apparently
been made on purpose for him. . . . No later than

Saturday afternoon — and early at that — Rutherford, having parted with the widower and seen him off the premises, ran upstairs to his wife's door, with a spring in his step and a light in his eyes that plainly showed *his* mourning to be over. Hilda was dead and gone, but Betty was alive in her splendid strength and beauty, and he was her husband and bridegroom, and his hour had come! The grave had closed over that broken heart, which had ached as long as it could feel, and ached most for him; but the world was still glorious for him and his love, and never so glorious as now. They began to bask in their happiness, as the house in the sunshine that flooded it, now that the blinds were drawn up. The shadow of death, close and terrible as it was, could not dim it for them any more.

In all the novels there are memorable scenes of tenderness, among the best of which are those between Fidelia and Adam Drewe, first in their brief meetings as girl and youth—she with her weak eyes bandaged, but reading him through his voice and bashful deprecation; he yearning to remain with her, but forcing himself away—and then in long years after, when he returns to find her in widowhood and poverty, and to all seeming hopelessly blind.

The conception of the latter scene is quite the best to be found in the whole of Ada

Cambridge's work, and has not been equalled in its kind by any other Australian writer. The simplicity and verbal reticence of this chapter of intense feeling gives also a good sample of the author's style of expression. Seldom ornate or much studied, it is ever a lucid and easy style. As a narrative specimen, the following, from the same novel, is conveniently quotable :

It was not much of an accident, but it was enough. The engine buried its fore-paws in the soft earth of the embankment, where engines were not meant to go, and then paused abruptly in the attitude of a little dog hiding a bone in a flower-bed; the embankment sloped down instead of up, and the monster hung upon the edge of it, nose to the ground and hind-quarters in the air, looking as if a baby's touch would send it over. Several carriages, violently running upon it and being checked suddenly, stood on tip-toes, so to speak, and fell into each other's arms with a vehemence that completely overset them ; one rolled right down the bank, head first, and the others tumbled upon its kicking wheels. It was all over in a moment ; and the dazed passengers, realising in a second moment that the end of the world was still an event in the future, picked themselves up as best they could. No one was killed, but some were badly shaken, and most of them screamed horribly. The sound of those screams, mingled with the clanking and crashing of riven wood and metal, and the hissing of escaping steam, conveyed the idea of such an appalling catastrophe as would make history for the world.

Though not a satirist—she does not hate well enough to be that—Ada Cambridge has occasionally a neat and forcible way of describing character. Richard Delavel's first wife was 'a gentle and complaisant being, soft and smooth, apparently yielding to the touch, but dense, square, and solid as a well-dumped wool-bale.' When opposed in will or contradicted in her opinion, she smiled resignedly, and, if it appeared due to her dignity, sulked for a period. Yet generally she was 'the evenest-tempered woman that ever a well-meaning husband found it difficult to get on with.' A pattern of order and conscientiousness, 'governed by principles that were as correct as her manners and costume, and as firmly established as the everlasting hills,' she might have made an admirable wife for a clergyman, but was totally unsuited to Delavel, as he to her.

Still, she was very proud of the look of 'blood' in her Richard, and when he became wealthy, and she a fashionable hostess in

Sydney society, nothing delighted her more
than her opportunities of making the aristocratic connection known. Her own origin
as the daughter of a farmer was quite
forgotten. 'Annie might have been a
Delavel from the beginning, in her own
right, for all the recollection that remained
to her of the real character of her bringing
up. . . . Years and certain circumstances
will often affect a woman's memory that way
—a man somehow manages to keep a better
grasp of facts.'

Yelverton, the lover of Elizabeth King,
an English aristocrat spending some of his
wealth in lessening the misery and vice of
London, was 'not the orthodox philanthropist,
the half-feminine, half-neuter specialist with
a hobby, the foot-rule reformer, the prig with
a mission to set the world right ; his benevo-
lence was simply the natural expression of a
sense of sympathy and brotherhood between
him and his fellows, and the spirit which
produced that was not limited in any direction.'

His friend, Major Duff-Scott, 'an ex-officer of dragoons, and a late prominent public man of his colony (he was prominent still, but for his social and not his official qualifications), was a well-dressed and well-preserved old gentleman who, having sown a large and miscellaneous crop of wild oats in the course of a long career, had been rewarded with great wealth, and all the privileges of the highest respectability.'

ADAM LINDSAY GORDON.

THE strongest note of Adam Lindsay Gordon's poetry is a personal one. When he represents Australia best, he best represents his own striking character. Yet that character had clearly shown itself, as had also his lyric gift, before he saw Australia. He is the favourite poet of the country by a happy fortuity rather than by the merit of special native inspiration. Those tastes of the people which he has expressed in manner and degree so rare as to make a parallel difficult of conception were also his own dominant tastes. From early boyhood they had controlled his life, and in the end they wrecked it.

That any man living an adventurous and precarious life, often in rude associations and without the stimulus of ambition or of intellectual society, should write poetry at all is a matter for some wonder. And when several of the compositions of such a writer are marked by rare vigour and melody, and some few are worthy to rank with the best of their kind produced in the century, it must be held that the gift of the author is genuine and spontaneous. It is impossible to believe that Gordon would have been less a poet had he never lived under the Southern Cross; that he would have cared less for horses and wild riding, for manliness and the exhilaration of danger. Had he become a country gentleman in England, or a soldier, like his father, should we not still have had ' The Rhyme of Joyous Garde,' 'The Romance of Britomarte,' ' By Flood and Field,' and ' How we beat the Favourite.' And do these not form the majority of his best poems? A man apt alike for the risks of the chase or the cavalry charge, with a delicate ear for the music of words, with natural promptings to write, would in any conditions have found time to celebrate the things which his daring and gallant spirit loved. Had he not ridden as well as written the rides related by his 'Sick Stockrider,' he might have been foremost in that more glorious one so often present to his fiery fancy, and have wielded

'The splendid bare sword
Flashing blue, rising red from the blow!'

Gordon was a true soldier in sentiment all his life, as he was also a true Englishman, and it is the soldier and the Englishman in him far more than the Australian that the people of his adopted country, consciously or unconsciously, admire. It is yet difficult to consider his work as a writer apart from his personality. And it is natural that this should be so in the case of a man whose career was itself a romance, who led as strange a double life as ever poet lived, and who, through all, retained the marked essentials of a gentleman.

In his character as a sportsman and a rider there is an element of the ideal which largely helps to commend him to the majority of Australians. Though his liking for horses and the turf became a destroying passion, there was never anything sordid in it. He was not a gambler, for long after he had won recognition as the first steeplechase rider in a country of accomplished riders, he declined payment for his services on the race-track, accepting it only when compelled at last by poverty to do so ; and the distaste with which he had always viewed the meaner associations of the sport latterly became dislike and scorn. In the period of disappointment that preceded his death he refused a remunerative post on the sporting staff of a leading Melbourne journal because he wished to dissociate himself completely and finally from everything connected with the professionalism of sport.

As a Bush rider he became noted for the performance of feats which no one else would think of attempting. The Australians often speak and write of it as courage—absence of fear—but it surely had a large admixture of pure recklessness. It is at least evident that danger had a certain irresistible fascination for him. 'Name a jump, and he was on fire to ride at it,' is the description given of this

curious predilection which made his company
in a riding party a somewhat exciting pleasure.
The day in 1868 when he won three steeplechases at Melbourne is still remembered ;
and at Mount Gambier, in South Australia,
a granite obelisk marks where once he leaped
his horse over a fence surmounting the head-
land of a lake, and then across a chasm 'more
than forty feet wide.' A single false step
would have cast horse and rider into the lake
two hundred feet below. Of the same wild
character was his riding during boyhood in
the hunting-fields of Gloucestershire. It
would be natural to suspect some measure of
vanity or bravado in all this, but no hint of
either is given by any of his acquaintances ;
and the few who knew him well are emphatic
in placing him, as a man and a sportsman,
apart from and above the majority of those
with whom the conditions of his life brought
him into contact. 'Gordon,' says one of his
intimate friends, ' was always a quiet, modest,
pure-minded gentleman. . . . I never knew
such a noble-hearted man, especially where
women were concerned.'

The deep melancholy in many of Gordon's poems has been attributed to the influence of Australian scenery, and to the loneliness of the earlier years of his life in the colonies. This explanation, if not wholly erroneous, is at least much exaggerated. It ignores the most obvious elements of the poet's temperament. It takes no account of the history of wasted opportunities and regrets, of defeat and discontent, of self-wrought failure and remorse, that may plainly be read in 'To my Sister,' 'An Exile's Farewell,' 'Early Adieux,' 'Whispering in the Wattle Boughs,' 'Quare Fatigasti,' 'Wormwood and Nightshade,' and other poems. The writer, as he himself says, has no reserve in the criticism of his own career.

> 'Let those who will their failings mask,
>   To mine I frankly own ;
> But for their pardon I will ask
>   Of none—save Heaven alone.'

Gordon's youth was wild and ungoverned. Before his twenty-first year his folly had lost him home, friends, love, and the one profession that might have steadied him, as well as afforded him distinction. He was the son of Captain Adam D. Gordon (an officer who had seen service in India) and the grandson of a wealthy Scotch merchant. Captain Gordon settled at Cheltenham in the later years of his life, and intended that his son should study for the army; but a mad wilfulness and passion for outdoor sport had taken possession of the youth, and nothing could be done with him. He rode to hounds with all the daring that marked his horsemanship in later life; he rode in steeplechases, he frequented the company of pugilists at country fairs and public-houses, and joined in their contests; he was removed from two schools for unruly conduct, and a more serious escapade, though innocent of any bad intention, nearly caused his arrest by the police. At last it was agreed that he should emigrate to Australia. He was glad to go, but bitter at the thought of what his going implied. The knowledge that he suffered solely through his own fault did not make less disagreeable to him the censure of others, even that of the gallant father whom, in his wildest moments

of rebellion, he never ceased to love and
admire. The unhappiness attending this
severance from the home that he felt he
would never see again is told in a poem to
his sister, written (August, 1853) a few days
before he sailed.

'Across the trackless seas I go,
　No matter when or where;
And few my future lot will know,
　And fewer still will care.
My hopes are gone, my time is spent,
　I little heed their loss,
And if I cannot feel content,
　I cannot feel remorse.

'My parents bid me cross the flood,
　My kindred frowned at me;
They say I have belied my blood,
　And stained my pedigree.
But I must turn from those who chide,
　And laugh at those who frown;
I cannot quench my stubborn pride,
　Or keep my spirits down.

'I once had talents fit to win
　Success in life's career;
And if I chose a part of sin,
　My choice has cost me dear.

But those who brand me with disgrace,
　Will scarcely dare to say
They spoke the taunt before my face
　And went unscathed away.'

The stanzas (there are ten more in the poem) have all the bitterness of a youthful sorrow and all the vigour of a youthful defiance. But at the moment of his deepest depression it is upon himself that the writer casts the real blame. This is characteristic of his judgment of himself throughout life. He has ever too much honour and spirit to shirk the responsibility of his own acts. And the same qualities keep him from doing injury to others. He is consoled by remembering this in bidding good-bye to his native land.

'If to error I incline,
Truth whispers comfort strong,
That never reckless act of mine
E'er worked a comrade wrong.'

As a colonist, Gordon might have justified his Scotch descent by making a fortune. Wealth was to be gained in other and surer ways than by groping for it in the goldfields. But he was indifferent, and allowed himself to drift. Australia was attractive to him only as a place of adventure, of freedom, of retirement, of oblivion. All but the latter he found it. He readily adapted himself to the rough conditions of the country, but could never overcome the thought that in those first false steps he had lost all worth striving for. Time softened the gloomy defiance of his farewell verses, but did not alter his determination to efface himself, to be forgotten even by his family. He held no communication with anyone in England, and heard nothing from his home until ten years later, when a lawyer's letter notified him that both his mother and father were dead, and that under the will of the latter he was to receive a legacy of seven thousand pounds. Meanwhile, Gordon appears to have made no attempt to win any of the prizes that were the common reward of pluck and industry in the Australia of the fifties. He joined the mounted police force of South Australia, but, impatient of its discipline, soon left it, and for long afterwards was content with the rough employment of a horse-breaker.

A curious, pathetic figure he makes at this time. He broke in horses during the day, and read the classic poets at night. Think of the refined Englishman in blue blouse, fustian, and half-Wellington boots, seated among the boisterous company of a 'men's hut' on a Bush station, reading Horace by the aid of a rude lamp, 'consisting of a honeysuckle cone stuck in clay in a pannikin, and surrounded with mutton fat!' Or sitting at some Bush camp of his own, and imagining, as he so finely did, the famous Balaclava Charge, which set Europe ringing with pity and admiration a year after he arrived in Australia. How he would have liked to be among the actors in that scene!

> 'Oh! the minutes of yonder maddening ride
> Long years of pleasure outvie!'

he exclaims, and wishes that his own end could be fair as that of one 'who died in his stirrups there.'

Gordon seemed not only to be reconciled to his Bush life, but to have become attached to it. He once declared it to be better in

many respects than any other.   He was
temperate, skilful in his work, and as popular
as one of reserved manner can be.   Most
of the squatters of the period made it a
practice to receive into their social circle any
companionable and educated man, whether
their equal in position or not.   It was a
generous custom, typical of the most hos-
pitable country in the world, and worked
well on the whole.   But Gordon, unlike
Henry Kingsley and others of the same
class, took no advantage of it.   That the
squatters did not themselves recognise the
worth of one so unassertive was not to be
wondered at.   He saw this, and never blamed
them.   They could not, as he remarked on
one occasion, be expected to know that he
was as well born as any of them, and perhaps
better educated.   One of them saw there was
'something above the common' in him ; but
that was all.   At length he was discovered
by a good-natured and scholarly Roman
Catholic priest (the Rev. Julian E. Tenison
Woods), who, though he does not say so,
evidently took a pleasure during the five

years of their acquaintance in making the
merits of the solitary Englishman known in
the colony. Their tastes accorded excellently.
They talked 'horses or poetry' as they rode
together, or smoked by their camp-fires.
Gordon's reserve thawed for the first time.
He had a well-trained memory, and occasionally would recite Latin or Greek verse,
or a scene from Shakespeare, or passages
from Byron and other modern poets. Greek
he had taught himself in lonely hours after
his arrival in Australia, having neglected it
while at college.

In the end his disposition left the good
cleric, like many another, much puzzled.
Was there anything of foolish pride or
misanthropy in Gordon's avoidance of society
that would have welcomed him? Both his
recorded speech and his poems are without
evidence of either. Those who remember
his taciturnity and little eccentricities also
speak of his kindness of heart, generosity
and trustfulness of others. Did he ever
complain that he was oppressed and saddened
by his self-chosen life in the Bush? We have

seen the high estimate he once gave of it ;
and Mr. Woods, who has recorded many
proofs of close observation of his friend,
testifies that the melancholy of his poems
found little or no expression in his conversation. Gordon may have been shy (as Marcus
Clarke noted), but he early formed a fairly
accurate judgment of his literary powers. He
said ' he was sure he would rise to the top of
the tree in poetry, and that the world should
talk of him before he died.' Coming from
one who was far from being vain or boastful,
the remark suggests hope and ambition. But
neither, it would seem from his colonial
career, was ever more than a passing mood
with him. Why did he remain in obscurity
during several of the best years of his life,
doing rough and dangerous work, when he
might have obtained some remunerative post
in one of the cities ? Why did he marry a
domestic servant—one who could never be
an intellectual companion for him ?

It appears that he considered himself to
have 'irretrievably lost caste.' It is a
fantastic idea, and could not have any justifi-

cation in a country where an Englishman of good manners and behaviour need never want congenial society. Gordon was abnormally proud, independent and sensitive : an unfortunate disposition for anyone who has his way to make in an imperfect world. Such a man constantly misunderstands himself and is misunderstood. He takes severe, unpractical views of his own character and of life generally. Not necessarily morose or ungenial, he is always apt to be thought so. Gordon's conclusion that he had lost caste is a proof of supersensitiveness, and the deep effect produced upon his temperament by the incidents of his youth.

There is a touching and significant little story of an acquaintance which he formed with a young lady at Cape Northumberland, and how he ended it. We are delicately told that, having become a warm admirer of his dashing horsemanship, the lady used to walk in early morning to a neighbouring field to see him training a favourite mare over hurdles. Something more than a mutual liking for horses and racing is plainly

hinted at as existing between them.   But
after they had met thus a few times, Gordon
asked abruptly whether her mother knew
that she came there every morning to see
him ride. She replied in the negative, adding
that her mother disapproved of racing.
'Well, don't come again,' said he ; 'I know
the world, and you don't. Good-bye. Don't
come again.' Surprised and wounded, the
lady silently gave him her hand in farewell.
'He looked at it as if it were some natural
curiosity, and said, " It's the first time I have
touched a lady's hand for many a day—my
own fault, my own fault—good-bye."'

For a brief period after the receipt of his
father's legacy Gordon looked towards his
future with some interest and confidence.
He spoke of a proposal to undertake regular
journalistic work at Melbourne, and to make
an attempt at writing novels. It was at this
time also that he foresaw that he would make
a name as a poet. The people of Mount
Gambier, finding him presently settled as the
owner of a small estate in the district, made
him their representative in the Legislative

Assembly of South Australia. In this new character he seems to have achieved only a reputation for drawing humorous sketches. Having delivered a few speeches highly embellished with classical allusions which failed to make any impression upon the plain business men of the House, he subsided, and was afterwards seldom heard. And when his seat became vacant in due course, he did not seek re-election. He had been unable to take his Parliamentary experience seriously. He is said to have always looked back upon it as something of a joke.

And now, with a revival of his former attachment to the excitements and uncertainties of the turf, begin a series of misfortunes which pursued him until his death. His property, mismanaged and neglected, had to be sold, and he set out a poor man once more for the adjoining colony of Victoria. Here, while suffering ill-health and poverty—starving in his own proud way—after failing in a small business which he had undertaken, Gordon learned that he would probably come into possession of the barony of Esselmont in Scotland, then producing an income of about two thousand pounds a year. But on further inquiry it was found that his title to the estate ceased with the abolition of the entail under the Entail Amendment Act of 1848. The excitement of his ill-fortune and the effects of a recent wound on the head combined to unhinge his mind, and in June, 1870, at the age of thirty-seven he ended his life by shooting himself at Brighton, near Melbourne. In comparing the impressions of Gordon's disposition given by his friends, it is curious to note that among the few things in which they agree is an absence of surprise at his suicide.

It would not be difficult to imagine a more representative poet in the provincial sense than Gordon. His description of the colonies as

> 'Lands where bright blossoms are scentless,
> And songless bright birds,'

would be strangely misleading were it not contradicted by other lines from the same hand, showing a delicate appreciation of the rugged features of Australian scenery. But he sees them only in passing, or as a symbol of something he is pondering, or as a contrast to what he has left behind 'on far English ground.' No sight or sound of Australian Nature is a sole subject of any of his poems. His 'Whispering in the Wattle Boughs' does not express the voices of the forest, but the echoes of a sad youth, the yearnings of an exile ; his 'Song of Autumn' is not a song of autumn, but a forecast of his own death—a forecast that was fulfilled. If he ever felt any enthusiasm for the future nationhood of Australia, he did not express it. And such few native legends as there were, he left to other pens.

In all of his best poems, there is some central human interest, something that tells for courage, honour, manly resignation. When a story does not come readily to his hand in the new world, he seeks one in the old. He fondly turns to the spacious days of the old knighthood, when men drank and loved deeply, when they were ready to put happiness or life itself upon a single hazard. The subjects that Gordon best liked were short dramatic romances, which he found it easier to evolve from literature than from the life and history of his adopted country. Beyond the compositions upon the national sport of horse-racing, the only noteworthy Australian subjects in his three slender volumes are 'The Sick Stockrider's Review of the Excitements and Pleasures of a Careless Bush Life, and his Pathetic Self-satisfaction'; 'The Story of a Shipwreck'; 'Wolf and Hound,' which describes a duel between the hunted-down bushranger and a trooper; and some verses on the death of the explorer Burke. 'Ashtaroth,' an elaborate attempt at a sustained dramatic lyric in the manner of Goethe's 'Faust' and 'Manfred,' fills one of the three volumes, and among shorter pieces in the other two are more than a dozen suggested by the poet's reading, by his recollections of English life, and, in a notable instance, by one of the most memorable of modern European wars.

In a dedication prefixed to the *Bush Ballads*, Gordon suggests some of the local sources of his inspiration. He obviously overstates his obligations to the country.

Some of the best of the poems in this,
the most characteristic collection of his work,
have no association with it whatever. 'The
Sick Stockrider,' 'From the Wreck,' and
'Wolf and Hound' are colonial experiences,
finely described. But most of the remaining
poems, while they owe something to Tennyson, Browning, and Swinburne, are not in
any sense Australian.

> ' In the Spring, when the wattle gold trembles
>   'Twixt shadow and shine,
> When each dew-laden air resembles
>   A long draught of wine,
> When the skyline's blue burnished resistance
> Makes deeper the dreamiest distance,
> Some songs in all hearts have existence :
>   Such songs have been mine.'

But where, save in the retrospect of ' The
Sick Stockrider ' and a verse or two of ' From
the Wreck,' shall we find any of the air of
the lovely, transient Australian spring ? It
is rather absurd to place with *Bush Ballads*
the ' Rhyme of Joyous Garde,' a recital of
the old tragedy of Arthur and Launcelot ;
the story of seventeenth-century siege and
gallantry in the ' Romance of Britomarte ';

the dramatic scenes from the ' Road to Aver-
nus ;' ' The Friends ' (a translation from the
French) ; and the psychological musings of
' De Te ' and ' Doubtful Dreams.'

And the galloping rhymes ?　Yes, there
is indeed one galloping rhyme—' How we
beat the Favourite '—with a ring and a rush,
a spirit and swiftness of colour, not approached by the best verse of Egerton War-
burton or Whyte-Melville.　Especially vivid
and terse is the description of the latter part
of the race, where the favourite (The Clown)
overtakes Iseult, the mare leading in the run
home.

' She rose when I hit her.　I saw the stream glitter,
　　A wide scarlet nostril flashed close to my knee ;
Between sky and water The Clown came and caught her;
　　The space that he cleared was a caution to see.

' And forcing the running, discarding all cunning,
　　A length to the front went the rider in green ;
A long strip of stubble, and then the big double,
　　Two stiff flights of rails with a quickset between.

' She raced at the rasper, I felt my knees grasp her,
　　I found my hands give to the strain on the bit ;
She rose when The Clown did — our silks as we
　　bounded
Brushed lightly, our stirrups clashed loud as we lit.

'A rise steeply sloping, a fence with stone coping,
    The last—we diverged round the base of the hill ;
His path was the nearer, his leap was the clearer,
    I flogged up the straight, and he led sitting still.

'She came to his quarter, and on still I brought her,
    And up to his girth, to his breast-plate she drew ;
A short prayer from Neville just reached me, "'The
        Devil !"
    He muttered—lock'd level the hurdles we flew.'

After a glance at the crowd where, as seen
by the rider, all 'figures are blended and
features are blurred '—

'On still past the gateway she strains in the straight way,
    Still struggles, "The Clown by a short neck at
        most !"
He swerves, the green scourges, the stand rocks and
        surges,
    And flashes, and verges, and flits the white post.

'Aye ! so ends the tussle—I knew the tan muzzle
    Was first, though the ring men were yelling " Dead
        Heat !"
A nose I could swear by, but Clarke said "The mare
        by
    A short head." And that's how the favourite was
        beat.'

It was by this piece, according to Marcus
Clarke, that the poet's early reputation was
made. 'Intensely nervous, and feeling much

of that shame at the exercise of the higher
intelligence which besets those who are
known to be renowned in field sports,
Gordon produced his poems shyly, scribbled
them on scraps of paper, and sent them
anonymously to magazines.   It was not
until he discovered one morning that everybody knew a couplet or two of " How we
beat the Favourite" that he consented to
forego his anonymity and appear in the unsuspected character of a verse-maker.'   Even
in this picture of the excitements of the turf,
there is nothing that would not be as true of
Epsom or Ascot as of Randwick or Fleming-
ton.   Yet, it *is* Australian in the sense that it
expresses the one taste which, of all those inherited by the people from their British
ancestors, seems never likely to be lost (as
it was by the American colonists)—which,
on the contrary, has gained in ardour in the
new land.   Gordon was a pronounced
believer in the efficacy of field sports as a
means of maintaining the nerve and hardi-
hood of the race.   In one of his minor pieces
he vigorously affirms that

'If once we efface the joys of the chase
    From the land, and out-root the Stud,
Good-bye to the Anglo-Saxon Race,
    Farewell to the Norman Blood.'

With him the fearless huntsman makes the fearless soldier. Both are to be cultivated and admired, and when the latter dies needlessly, as at Balaclava, we are to be none the less proud of him,

'As a type of our chivalry.'

Of the longer poems, the two best in artistic quality are 'The Rhyme of Joyous Garde' and 'The Sick Stockrider.' They afford a complete contrast in subject, tone and treatment. The old Arthurian story is the finer and more finished. There is a nobility in its expression not elsewhere equalled by the author. But the other poem is more direct and simple in its pathos, more easily understood. It tells something of familiar experience in language irresistibly touching and musical. It would be interesting and a favourite if only through the obvious fact that it describes in part some of Gordon's own early life.

‘ ”Twas merry in the glowing morn, among the gleaming
    grass
    To wander as we’ve wandered many a mile,
And blow the cool tobacco cloud, and watch the white
    wreaths pass,
    Sitting loosely in the saddle all the while.
”Twas merry ’mid the backwoods, when we spied the
    station roofs,
    To wheel the wild-scrub cattle at the yard,
With a running fire of stockwhips and a fiery run of
    hoofs ;
    Oh ! the hardest day was never then too hard.

‘ Aye ! we had a glorious gallop after Starlight and his
    gang,
    When they bolted from Sylvester’s on the flat ;
How the sun-dried reed-beds crackled, how the flint-
    strewn ranges rang
    To the strokes of Mountaineer and Acrobat !
Hard behind them in the timber, harder still across
    the heath,
    Close beside them through the ti-tree scrub we
    dashed ;
And the golden-tinted fern-leaves, how they rustled
    underneath !
    And the honeysuckle osiers, how they crashed !’

‘ The Rhyme of Joyous Garde’ loses in
appreciation by assuming familiarity on the
part of the reader with all the details of the
story.   It is too allusive.   It is a description

more of Launcelot's remorse than of the crime which occasions it. As to the other classic themes, they probably avail as little to the reputation of the author as did the elegant quotations which he inflicted upon the South Australian legislators. ' He talked of the Danai, whilst they were vastly more interested in the land valuators.'

Gordon's work was introduced to the English public by an article in *Temple Bar* in 1884, and in 1888 a short memoir of him, entitled *The Laureate of the Centaurs* (now out of print), was published. Since then his poems have become known throughout the English-speaking world. Is this because he is called an Australian poet—because people wish to learn something of Australian life from his pages? Do English readers ever ask for the poems of Harpur, or Henry Kendall, or Brunton Stephens? No; Gordon's poems are admired for the human interest in them; for what they tell of tastes and personal qualities dear to the pleasure-loving and fighting Briton in whatever land he may be. It is the sort of admiration that

finds fit expression when an English officer
and artist makes a present to the publishers
of a spirited and valuable set of drawings to
illustrate the poem of the Balaclava Charge.
No other Australian poet has yet found
entrance to the great popular libraries of
England. Kendall, who almost deserves to
be called the Australian Shelley, tells more
of Nature in one of his graceful pages than
can be found in a volume of his contemporary.
But his thoughts are too remote from the
common interests of life ; and of his own
character he has recorded only what is sad
and painful. For the rest, his brief history
seems to prove that scarce any service may
be less noticed or thanked in Australia than
the describing of its natural beauties or the
writing of its national odes.

Gordon has more than once been mis-
represented with respect to his religious
views. He has been called an agnostic, an
atheist, even a pagan. Passages in nearly a
score of his poems must be read and compared before an opinion can properly be
given on the point. That he was a doubter,

and to some extent a fatalist, appears certain ;
but there is nothing to support the charge of
atheism. He shows a very clear conception
of the Christian ideas respecting right and
wrong, and of the Divine mercy, but hesitates
to accept any theories of punishment in a
future state. His general attitude is one of
hope, and of desire to believe. He often
thinks—too often—of the transciency of life,
and of the question to be solved 'beyond the
dark beneath the dust.' But there is no
despair. And meanwhile his practical creed is

> ' Question not, but live and labour
>   Till yon goal be won,
> Helping every feeble neighbour,
>   Seeking help from none.
> Life is mostly froth and bubble,
>   Two things stand like stone—
> KINDNESS in another's trouble,
>   COURAGE in your own.'

It conveys at once the highest and truest
of the many views he has given of his own
character. Generous to others, he was too
seldom just to himself. It was well there
remained among the friends he left behind a
few who knew him for what he was, and who

were unwilling that qualities often clouded
during his life by an unhappy temperament
should be undervalued or forgotten. Kendall's
' In Memoriam ' is a worthy tribute, and
finely summarizes the general impression of
Gordon which one obtains from his verse :

' The bard, the scholar, and the man who lived
That frank, that open-hearted life which keeps
The splendid fire of English chivalry
From dying out ; the one who never wronged
A fellow-man ; the faithful friend who judged
The many anxious to be loved of him
By what he saw, and not by what he heard,
As lesser spirits do ; the brave great soul
That never told a lie, or turned aside
To fly from danger ; he, I say, was one
Of that bright company this sin-stained world
Can ill afford to lose.'

ROLF BOLDREWOOD.

ENGLISH readers of Rolf Boldrewood's novels have often wondered why he has ignored in his writings the modern social life of Australia. He has a unique knowledge of the country extending over sixty years, but his literary materials have been drawn only from the first half of this period. No other purely Australian novelist has succeeded in making a considerable reputation without feeling the necessity of fleeing to the more congenial atmosphere of literary London.

It is true that even he had to find acceptance at home through the circuitous route of the press and the libraries of Great Britain, but he was able to wait for his long-delayed popularity, and when it came and found him in advanced age, he had no inclination to leave the land of his adoption. Probably if literature had been to him more of a profession and less of a taste and pastime, he would long ago have felt inclined to turn his back upon the indifference with which the colonies usually treat their own products in authorship until English approval has imparted new virtues to them.

Most of the other writers who have contributed to the portrayal of a certain few aspects of Antipodean life have gone to London or elsewhere. Many years absent from Australia, they know little of its later developments. Boldrewood has spent a long and eventful life there. Of the southern half of the continent he must possess a specially intimate knowledge. Melbourne he has known in all the stages of its growth from a canvas-built hamlet to the finest city in the Southern Hemisphere. When he saw it first, the great golden wealth of the country lay unsuspected, and Ballarat and Bendigo were not.

Though English by birth, he is wholly Australian in training and experience. In

1830, being then four years old, he was taken by his parents to Sydney, and there educated. Early in youth he became one of the pioneer squatters of Western Victoria, sharing with a few others the danger of dispossessing the aboriginals, and soon acquiring considerable wealth. But some years later, going back to New South Wales, and venturing to establish himself there on a larger scale as a sheep-owner, he was involved in a disastrous drought and lost nearly everything.

In *The Squatter's Dream*, which is understood to be partly autobiographical, he has minutely recorded the varying fortunes of pastoral life in the colonies. But the bitterness of failure never caused him to forget the happiness of his young enthusiasm, or to speak ill of a pursuit so much identified with the prosperity of the country. He refers to it as 'that freest of all free lives, that pleasantest of all pleasant professions—the calling of a squatter.'

Abandoning his ambition to rank with the wool-kings, he entered the Civil Service as a police magistrate and gold-fields com-

missioner. In these combined offices he
spent twenty-five years, and, while continuing
a good public servant, contrived, like Anthony
Trollope, to find time for substantial work in
literature. Though during a period of about
twenty years he contributed several stories
and other literary matter to the Sydney and
Melbourne press, it was not until the publication of *Robbery under Arms*, at London in
1889, that his work obtained due recognition
even in the colonies. Ten years earlier he
had made an unsuccessful bid for an English
reputation by the publication of *Ups and
Downs*, the novel which, under the more
attractive title of *The Squatter's Dream*,
reappeared in 1890 as a successor to the
famous bushranging story. That the spirited
opening chapters of *Robbery under Arms*
should have been thought lightly of by
Australian editors when the serial rights of
the story were offered to them is somewhat
astonishing. The author has related how
these chapters were successively rejected by
a number of the leading journals, including
two of the best weeklies.

At length the manuscript was read by Mr. Hugh George, manager of the *Sydney Morning Herald* and the *Sydney Mail*, who promptly accepted it for publication in the latter newspaper.

Boldrewood at this time (1880) was well known to the Australian press. It must, however, be pointed out in justice to the editors, whom his story failed to impress, that his previous work had revealed little of the dramatic sense that contributed so materially to his success in presenting the careers of his highwaymen. But it is less easy to see why, when the full possibilities of the story had been realised, there should have remained a second difficulty, that of securing a publisher to issue it in book form. 'An Australian house,' the author has said, 'refused to undertake the risk;' and he adds, 'as a matter of fact I had to publish it partly on my own account in England.' This proof of his confidence in the attractions of the story has since been justified by its complete success throughout the English-speaking world.

A writer with so much experience of
Australia, and continuing to reside in it,
cannot be surprised if he is expected to take
a large share of responsibility for the fact
that Australian fiction—the fiction produced
by writers known to the British public—only
in a slight degree reflects the most interesting
features in the present-day life of the country.
At the same time, no such considerations can
detract from the sterling merits of Rolf Boldrewood's actual services to Australian literature.
It is hardly possible to believe that the
English people still prefer to look to Australia only for stories of adventure ; but if
they do—and as the first to welcome and appreciate colonial writers they are perhaps entitled to exercise a choice—it is well that such
stories be written from complete local knowledge, and thus at least correctly describe the
broader aspects of the country.

If Boldrewood were asked to explain his
silence respecting Antipodean life of the
present day, he might reply that the novel
of modern manners did not form any part of
the work which he had chosen to do.   At

all events, he could claim to be as much a historian as a novelist. It has been his ambition to describe Australia chiefly as he saw it in his youth, about forty years ago— as it was immediately before and after the discovery of gold. That his record *per se* is strikingly vivid and faithful is the first general impression which his novels make upon the reader, whether English or colonial. There is about them much of that air of ' rightness ' which Hall Caine has noted to be one of the most enduring qualities of good fiction, whatever its literary style may be. They are cheerful, virile, soundly moral, and take far more account of the good than of the bad in human nature. There is no fondness of the sensational for its own sake. The conditions of probability are observed with a closeness which, in books dependent for their interest so largely upon plot and incident, amounts almost to a fault.

An English historian is said to have declared that he would willingly exchange a library full of the poets for a single good novel of the period in which he was interested. One can readily imagine that if a generation or two hence there should be any Australian history left unwritten, any unsatisfied curiosity concerning the simple annals now so familiar to us, Rolf Boldrewood's novels might be found, within their limits, a more satisfying source of information than all the rest of contemporary Australian literature combined, the formal chroniclers included, as well as the poets : that is to say, the general view they would furnish of certain features of pioneer life would be fuller and clearer, and, minor details apart, more reliable than could be gathered from any other source.

Where is there in the elaborate histories of Rusden, Lang, Blair, and Flanagan, or in any of the numerous books of sketches and reminiscences written by persons who have visited or temporarily resided in Australia, a view of the picturesque variety, colour, and splendid energy of the great first race for gold to compare with that given in the second volume of *The Miner's Right*, or with the memorable account of what Starlight and the Marstons saw at Turon during their temporary retirement from the highway?

Boldrewood, in these descriptions, has done what Henry Kingsley, with his more eloquent pen, if slighter personal experience, unaccountably neglected, and what Charles Reade, though he never saw Australia, vividly imagined, and regretted his inability to fully employ. Reade saw a theme for a great epic 'in the sudden return of a society far more complex, artificial, and conventional than Pericles ever dreamed of, to elements more primitive than Homer had to deal with; in this, with its novelty and nature and strange contrasts; in the old barbaric force and native colour of the passions as they burst out undisguised around the gold; in the hundred and one personal combats and trials of cunning; in a desert peopled and cities thinned by the magic of cupidity; in a huge army collected in ten thousand tents, not as heretofore by one man's constraining will, but each human unit spurred into the crowd by his own heart; in the "siege of gold" defended stoutly by rock and disease; in the world-wide effect of the discovery, the peopling of the earth at last according to Heaven's long-published and resisted design.'

If Boldrewood had not himself realized the literary value of the stirring scenes in which his youth was passed, this summary of the English novelist, published in 1856, might well have suggested it to him. How far has he succeeded in commemorating those scenes, and in what directions chiefly ?

In the first place, it is the pictorial, the literal, not the philosophical, aspect of the subject which has most attracted him. There is a personal zest in his remembrance of the general animation of the scene, a keen sense of the pleasurable excitement, freedom and good-fellowship of the life. His books are essentially men's books. This is the universal report of the English libraries. Analytical subtleties there are none. Boldrewood is not given to weighing moonbeams. His nearest approach to psychology consists in noting the various effects of robust, unconventional colonial life upon fortune-seekers and visitors from the mother country. This

has been a favourite theme with all Australian
writers, and one of which the female novelists
have so far made the most effective use. One
could wish that Boldrewood had made himself as far as possible an exception to the
rule—that he had aimed at a praiseworthy
provinciality by matching with the elaborate
minuteness of his local colour some finished
and memorable studies of Australian character.

Maud Stangrove in *The Squatter's Dream*,
and Antonia Frankston in *The Colonial Reformer*, who seem to offer the best opportunities to typify Australian womanhood, are
gracefully described ; but, save for an occasional longing to relieve the monotony of
their lives by a taste of European travel and
culture, they are indistinguishable from such
purely English types as Ruth Allerton and
Estelle Challoner. Very pathetic, and marked
by some distinctively Antipodean traits, is
the sister of the bushrangers in *Robbery under
Arms*. Aileen Marston has the strong self-
reliance and independence which are born of
the exigencies, as well as of the free life, of

the country. She and her brothers represent much of what is best in Boldrewood's portrayal of native character. Maddie and Bella Barnes and Miss Falkland in the same novel, Kate Lawless in *Nevermore*, and Possie Barker in *A Sydneyside Saxon*, are also Antipodeans, but are only lightly sketched.

Boldrewood claims that in his writings he has always upheld the Australian character. It is a fact that he has incidentally done this to a considerable extent, but not by any notable portraiture. In the period with which the novels deal the population of the colonies was largely English; it was, therefore, perhaps only natural that the stranger and adventurer from the Old World, so often well born and cultured, should prove a more attractive study than the sons of the soil. Moreover, the latter, in their monotonous and circumscribed life, lacked much of the mystery and romance so vital to the novel of adventure. But when this has been admitted in Boldrewood's favour, there still remains a broader charge to which he is liable.

He has been accused, and it must be confessed with a good deal of justice, of paying too little attention in later novels (taking the order of their publication in London) to the development of even those characters most concerned in his plots. The fault is purely one of judgment. It is hardly possible to suppose any lack of ability in a writer who has produced the bright and suggestive dialogue scattered through the pages of *Robbery under Arms* and *The Miner's Right.* Giving rein to his passion for reminiscence and descriptive detail, he has paid the inevitable penalty of a loss in human interest. So obvious is this loss in the stories of pastoral life, that one is almost fain to assume it to be the result of deliberate choice. How far the author, in this section of his writing, has neglected the social and dramatic possibilities of country life, can be judged by noting Mrs. Campbell Praed's work in *The Head Station, Policy and Passion,* or *The Romance of a Station.* But the best contrast to Boldrewood's style is furnished by the author of *Geoffry Hamlyn.*

Henry Kingsley decided the movement of

his characters with a loving care. Their interests were paramount to him. They made their own story; the story did not make them. Their author cared little for the externals of Australian life except in so far as they helped to tell something, especially something good, of his leading personages. His interest in them was not semi-scientific, like that of Thackeray or Jane Austen, Howells or Henry James, in their studies of human nature; it was that mainly of a sympathiser and a partisan.

His frequently expressed anxiety about the impression they were making upon the reader was not always an affectation. There is a real solicitude in the confidences concerning William Ravenshoe upon his sudden promotion from the stable to the drawing-room of Ravenshoe Manor. 'I hope you like this fellow, William,' he says in one place, and then there is a naïve enumeration of some of the ex-groom's social deficiencies. This, at best, is a useless interruption of the story, but it helps, with other signs, to show Kingsley's constant interest in his characters.

Nearly everything in his descriptions of Australian squatting pursuits is intended to have a definite and notable bearing upon them. Thus, the view we get of the drafting-yard at Garoopna, with Sam Buckley in torn shirt, dust-covered, and wielding a deft pole on the noses of the terrified cattle, is not presented as a piece of station-life so much as a picturesque means of leading Alice Brentwood into an involuntary display of her affection for Sam when he is struck down before her eyes.

Again, the description of the kangaroo-hunt, given in the same novel, is remembered chiefly on account of the picture of Sam and Alice in the frank enjoyment of their first love as they loiter in the tracks of the sportsmen, and, relinquishing the chase with happy indifference, go home and sit together under the verandah.

Kingsley avoided the fault, common to his successors, of exaggerating the interest which readers are supposed to take in the general aspects of life in a new country. He had a keen sense of the value of picturesque environment, but wisely contrived that nothing should withdraw attention from the progress of his drama. He was ever on the watch for opportunities to sketch in lightly and humorously small traits of character, and to emphasise salient ones. ' She had an imperial sort of way of manœuvring a frying-pan,' he says, in allusion to the cheerful adaptability of the high-bred Agnes Buckley, that fine model of English womanhood, during her first rough experiences in Australia. When Hamlyn comes to Baroona from the neighbouring station to spend Christmas with his old friends, he finds the same lady ' picking raisins in the character of a duchess.' Considered apart from the story, these Dickensian touches might seem merely humorous exaggeration, but to those who have traced the development of Mrs. Buckley's character, how happy and pregnant they are !

Robbery under Arms not only contains Boldrewood's most dramatic plot, but his most skilful and sympathetic treatment of character. It is a distinct exception to the rest of his work. In the later stories the characters are brightly sketched, but with so casual a touch that they leave no permanent impression with the reader. The best excite no more than a passing admiration, whereas Kingsley's win lasting admiration and love. There can be no surer test of art and truth : it furnishes the one indubitable proof of clear vision, sympathy, and correct expression. Where the weakness of some of Boldrewood's characters is not due to deficiency of interest in them on the part of the author, it is the result of an attempt to copy life with an accuracy which sacrifices picturesqueness.

The attempt to preserve absolute truth in every detail of the life-story of John Redgrave, the hero of *The Squatter's Dream*, seems distinctly a case in point. In no other novel is there so complete a description of Australian squatting life—its varying success and failure, its solid comforts and wholesome happiness in times of prosperity. Redgrave is one of the most elaborately drawn of all the author's characters ; there is the fullest sense of probability in every incident ; the

entire story is plainly a direct transcript of
life ; nothing at first seems wanting. But
when the book is laid aside, the reader
realises that he has scarcely been once moved
by it. He has felt a transient pity for the
hero's misfortunes, and a mild satisfaction at
his modified ultimate success—nothing more.

The main defect here appears to consist in
the central motive of Redgrave's struggles
being limited to purely personal ambition.
His aim is no higher than that of a speculator
in a hurry to be rich, and when he fails, he
gets little more than the sympathy which is
commonly given to the man who plays for a
high stake and loses. His love for Maud
Stangrove, which might have been made a
controlling and ennobling influence, ranks
only as an incident. It comes after the main
impression of his character has been given.
Beyond doubt he represents a real type ; no
error has been made in this respect ; his
failure to win higher favour with us arises
from his too close approximation to the
common clay. There is absent just that
small element of the ideal with which even

the sternest of the apostles of realism in
letters have found it impracticable to dispense.

An illustration of how little Boldrewood
was inclined to idealise either his characters
or their surroundings is afforded by the
account of Redgrave's first visit to the home
of the Stangroves, his neighbours on the
Warroo. On the journey he passed a Bush
inn of the period where drunkenness was the
normal condition of everyone, from the owner
to the stable-boy. The shanty itself, an ugly
slab building roofed with corrugated iron,
'stood as if dropped on the edge of the bare
sandy plain.' It faced the dusty track which
did duty as a highroad ; at the back of the
slovenly yard was the river, chiefly used as a
receptacle for rubbish and broken bottles. A
half-score of gaunt, savage-looking pigs lay
in the verandah or stirred the dust and
bones in the immediate vicinity of the front-
entrance. 'What, in the name of wonder,'
inquired Jack of himself as he rode away,
'can a man do who lives in such a fragment
of Hades *but* drink?'

The home of the Stangroves, though less
depressing, bears painful evidence of its
isolation.   The settler's wife little resembles
Agnes Buckley—she is too typically colonial
for that.   'She was young, but a certain
worn look told of the early trials of matron-
hood.   Her face bore silent witness to the
toils of housekeeping with indifferent servants
or none at all ; to the want of average female
society ; to a little loneliness and a great deal
of monotony.'

The visitor meets another member of the
household, Stangrove's unmarried sister, a
beautiful and spirited young woman whose
impatience with her colourless life is out-
wardly subdued to ironical resignation.
'Another eventful day for Mr. Redgrave,'
she remarks on his return after a day's
riding over the station with her brother ;
'yesterday the sheep were lost—to-day the
sheep are found ; so passes our life on the
Warroo.'

The best argument against Boldrewood's
usual treatment of character is furnished by
the great bushranger chief who is the central

figure in *Robbery under Arms*. The author here submits for the first and only time to that fundamental law of fiction which demands a certain judicious exaggeration in the characters of a story depending for its interest mainly on the charm of circumstance. Starlight is at once the most real and least possible personage to be found in any of Boldrewood's novels. He becomes real because his character and actions are conceived in harmony with the romance and pathos of the story. Though it is obvious enough that there never could have existed a bushranger with quite so much of the *bel air*, or with a private code of honour so admirable, the exaggeration is far from obtrusive. He is of a stature suited to the deeds he performs, and, both he and his exploits being often closely associated with historical facts, a strong sense of reality is maintained.

Starlight seems to be a compound of several characters. He has Turpin's ubiquity, Claude Duval's *sang-froid*, the personal attractiveness of Gardiner (leader of a gang which made a business of robbing gold-

escorts in New South Wales about forty
years ago), and the humorous daredevilry of
the 'Captain Thunderbolt' who obtained
notoriety in the same colony a few years
later.

Boldrewood seems to have shrewdly agreed
with the dictum of Turpin, that it is necessary
for a highwayman, at all events a captain of
highwaymen, to be a gentleman. But Starlight, unlike Turpin, does not become vain
with success, and is far from being enamoured
with his profession. Indeed, he is quite with
the orthodox view of it. He is a bushranger,
apparently, because he no longer hopes or
desires to resume his rank in certain aristocratic circles from which, by occasional hints,
we are informed that he has fallen. He
indulges in no lugubrious moralisings—he is
far too agreeable a person for that—but
exhibits just the required touch of romance
by letting you know that in his past there is
a sadness which a career of excitement and
danger is necessary to enable him to forget.
Having been won over as a sympathiser and
admirer, the reader is ready to believe that

at worst the dashing outlaw could never have been a very bad fellow. Certainly the author has carefully kept him from participation in the grosser acts of lawlessness of which his revengeful old partner Ben Marston, the more typical bushranger, is guilty. Cattle-stealing and highway robbery as supervised by Starlight are allowable, and even meritorious, in so far as they afford him opportunities to practise some facetious deception on the police. Such raids are not crimes, but comedies.

There is excellent fun in his posing as 'Charles Carisforth, Esq., of Sturton, Yorkshire, and Banda, Waroona and Ebor Downs, N.S.W.,' while awaiting the arrival at Adelaide of the 1,100 head of stolen cattle, or as the 'Hon. Frank Haughton,' one of 'the three honourables' on the Turon gold-field. The rash daring and cleverness of these disguises furnish a combination of amusement and dramatic interest not approached in anything else that Boldrewood has written. Starlight's presence at dinner with the gold-fields commissioner and police magistrate at

Turon, when 'in walked Inspector Goring,'
the officer who had been so long and patiently
seeking him elsewhere, and his appearance
at Bella Barns' wedding, after a reward of
a thousand pounds has been offered for his
capture, are scenes which remain vivid in the
memory long after the more commonplace
adventures of the lords of Terrible Hollow
have lost their distinctness or been forgotten.

Next to his humour and courage, the
qualities which most endear this picturesque
marauder to the reader are the happy fierce-
ness with which he commands the respect of
his retainers, and his politeness and gallantry
to women. When a robbery is to be effected,
the plans are laid with sound generalship, but
there is no unnecessary violence or loss of
good manners. His conduct at the plunder-
ing of the gold-escort is fully equal to the
traditional suavity of Claude Duval. 'Now,
then, all aboard!' he calls out to the passengers when the contents of the coach have
been removed. 'Get in, gentlemen; our
business matters are concluded for the night.
Better luck next time! William, you had

better drive on. Send back from the next stage, and you will find the mail-bags under that tree. They shall not be injured more than can be helped.'

The bushranger of real life, as known to the pioneer colonist, would have bagged his booty with much fewer words. That Starlight should have 'treated all women as if they were duchesses,' and have made it a point of honour to keep his pledged word with them, in however slight a matter, seems only natural. Not even the women-folk of his enemy are allowed to want a protector. When Moran and his gang of ruffians take possession of Darjallook station during the absence of the male members of the household, Starlight and the Marstons ride twenty miles across country and rescue the ladies before the worst has been done. Starlight bows to them 'as if he was just coming into a ball-room,' and, retiring, raises Miss Falkland's hand to his lips like a knight of old.

These passages are only a few of the many which might be cited to show how far the author, fired with the spirit and romance of the story, gave freedom to his imagination in shaping the proportions of his leading character. Starlight, though he is not, and cannot be, a portrait of any single colonial outlaw of real life, is sufficiently natural to consistently represent in both his conduct and adventures much that was typical of Australian bushranging forty years ago and later.

Some of his characteristics, and at least one of the concluding episodes of the story, were suggested by the career of a New South Wales horse-stealer who became known as 'Captain Moonlight.' So much is certain. Boldrewood has himself narrated to a contributor of the Australian *Review of Reviews* his recollections of Moonlight and his end : 'Among other horses he stole was a mare called Locket, with a white patch on her neck. We had all seen her. This was the horse that brought about his downfall, and he was actually killed on the Queensland border in the way I have described in *Robbery under Arms*. Before that, Moonlight had had some encounters with Sergeant Wallings

(Goring); and this day, when Wallings rode straight at him, he said: "Keep back, if you're wise, Wallings. I don't want your blood on my head; but if you must——" But Wallings rode at him at a gallop. Two of the troopers fired point-blank at Moonlight, and both shots told. He never moved, but just lifted his rifle. Wallings threw up his arms, and fell off his horse a dying man. As Moonlight was sinking, the leader of the troopers said: "Now you may as well tell us what your name is." But he shook his head, and died with the secret.' He was 'a gentlemanly fellow,' probably one of that unhappy class of young Englishmen of good birth and no character who are exiled to the colonies for their sins, and there often acquire new vices or sink into obscurity.

When Archibald Forbes was in New Zealand a few years ago, he met a peer's son who was earning his 'tucker' as a station-cook. A Chinaman, aspiring to better things, had vacated the billet in his favour! It is interesting to note the use Boldrewood makes in his novel of the suggestion afforded by

the bushranger's concealment of his identity.
When Starlight is overcome in his last
attempt at escape, the curiosity long felt
concerning his past life seems for the third
time in the story about to be gratified. But
the reader is once more and finally disappointed. The bushranger has given his last
messages, and is dying with some of the
indifference to existence which has char-
acterised him throughout the story.

'I say, Morringer, do you remember the last pigeon-
match you and I shot in, at Hurlingham?'

'Why, good God!' says Sir Ferdinand, bending down,
and looking into his face. 'It can't be! Yes; by Jove!
it is——'

He spoke some name I couldn't catch, but Starlight
put a finger on his lips, and whispered :

'You won't tell, will you?   Say you won't.'

The other nodded.

He smiled just like his old self.

'Poor Aileen!' he said, quite faint. His head fell
back. Starlight was dead !

Boldrewood's characters, as he has said
himself, are constructed from many models.
And the Marstons are, it seems, the only
personages he has drawn solely from life.
Gardiner, with whom some readers have

identified Starlight, was, it is recorded,
'a man of prepossessing appearance and
plausible address, who had many friends
even among the settlers never suspected
of sympathy with criminals, while many of
the fair sex regarded him as a veritable
hero.'

That the romantic life of this noted
criminal furnished Boldrewood with some
material there cannot be any doubt, but the
fictitious bushranger is far from being in any
respect a mere copy of the real one. In
Starlight's relations with women, for instance,
there is nothing but what is manly and
honourable, whereas one of Gardiner's exploits was the seduction of a settler's wife,
a beautiful woman whom he induced to elope
with him to a remote district in Queensland.
And, further, none of the sensational incidents connected with his capture—his escape
under a legal technicality from the death-
penalty suffered by some of his associates,
his imprisonment for twelve years and subsequent exile—are made use of in the novel.

The narrative method adopted in *Robbery*

under Arms has so much contributed to the success of the story as to be worthy of some comparison with the ordinary style of the author. The limitations imposed by the choice of a narrator with no pretensions to education or sentiment, and writing in the first person, proved in this case salutary rather than disadvantageous. They repressed Boldrewood's usual tendency to excessive detail, and kept his attention closely fixed on the drama of the story.

The occasional deficiency of local colour and loss of effect in the grouping of the characters is more than compensated for by the racy piquancy of Dick Marston's vernacular, and the aspect, unrivalled in Australian literature, which his account affords of bushranging life from the bushranger's own point of view. In the truth with which this view is presented lies the strength and lasting merit of what might otherwise have been little better than a commonplace series of sensational episodes.

Starlight and the Marstons, as we see them, are reckless and dangerous criminals, but they are not exactly the 'bloodthirsty cowards' and 'murderers' known to the press and police of the period. The little they can plead in excuse for their lives is plainly stated, while no complaint is urged against their fate, or attempt made to obscure its obvious lesson. Grim old Ben Marston's career illustrates one of the results of the stupidly cruel system of transporting persons from England to the colonies for petty offences which in these days are punished by a slight fine, and his sons are types of a class who were far from being as irreclaimable as their offences made them appear. 'Men like us,' Dick Marston is once made to say, 'are only half-and-half bad, like a good many more in this world. They are partly tempted into doing wrong by opportunity, and kept back by circumstances from getting into the straight track afterwards.'

The examples given in the story of the aptness of this remark are often very touching. The poor Marston boys are indeed only half bad. Their better natures, seconded by the influence of a good mother and sister, are continually urging them to reformation, but for this there is no opportunity. The decision of their fate by the turn of a coin when the first great temptation comes is symbolical of the trifling causes to which the ruin of so many young Bushmen in the early days of squatting was traceable.

The personal observation strongly marked in all Boldrewood's novels has in *Robbery under Arms* its fullest, as well as most skilful, expression. As a squatter, the author had seen the practices of the cattle-thief, and learned his language. He had observed the extent to which idleness and a love of horse-flesh combined to fill the gaols of the country, and in later years this knowledge was confirmed in the course of his long experience as a magistrate. The judgment with which he presents the case of the young Marstons as types of a class is excelled only by the literary skill employed upon the character of their chief.

But there was no need to make Dick Marston so often emphasise the comfort of living 'on the square,' and the folly of ever doing otherwise. The story bears a self-evident moral. Humour there is in plenty, but the pathos of tragedy is the dominant, as it is the appropriate, tone of the book. In no respect has greater accuracy been attained than in the reproduction of the Australian vernacular, that odd compound of English, Irish, Scotch, and American phrases and inflexions, with its slender admixture of original terms. Visitors to Australia have praised the purity of the English spoken there by the middle classes. Mr. Froude, as late as 1885, found that ' no provincialism had yet developed itself,' but he wrote chiefly of what he had heard in the towns. It is in the country that the colonial dialect—if speech so largely imitative can yet be called a dialect —is most heard.

Among other interesting features in Dick Marston's narrative is the curious half-impersonal view which the outlaws take of the efforts made by the Government to capture them, and their strong dislike, on the other hand, to the private persons who competed with the police for the large rewards

offered.   This detail is as true to life as the
example of the sympathy and assistance
accorded the bushrangers by settlers in the
neighbourhood of their mountain retreat.

It was sympathy of this kind, combined
with bribery, which so protected the Kelly
gang as to involve the Government of
Victoria in an outlay of about one hundred
and fifteen thousand pounds before their
destruction could be accomplished.   Effective
literary use will be made at some time in the
future of the exploits of this last and most
daring of all the bushranging gangs, but
many years must elapse before the sordid
aspects of their career shall have been forgotten, and only its romance be left.   And
nothing short of genius will be required to
refine the rude proportions of Ned Kelly
into something like the gentlemanly exterior
of the dashing captain, the smooth gallant,
the humorist, philosopher, and quick-change
artist of *Robbery under Arms*.

In *The Miner's Right*, which ranks second
in popularity among Boldrewood's novels, the
personal narrative style is again adopted, but

with little effect of the kind produced by
Dick Marston's vivid directness in the earlier
novel.   Hereward Pole, the hero, is a
cultured Englishman, sensitive and senti-
mental, who keeps an eye upon humanity at
large, as well as upon the business of making
a fortune which has brought him to the
colonies.   Half of his record, though a
striking picture of the gold-fields, is not an
inherent part of the story of his own career.
Confined to their strictly just limits, the
events which combine to prolong his separation from the sweetheart whom he has left in
England could have been told in fifty pages.
But this would not have been all the author
wished.   He was satisfied with a slender
plot and a *dénouement* which can be guessed
almost from the outset as soon as he saw that
they would carry the glowing scenes and
episodes of diggings life with which his
memory was so richly stocked.   One cannot
believe but that, in this case, his slender
attention to the long-drawn thread of the
story was the outcome of choice.   Else where
was the need for elaborateness in such details

as the dispute over the Liberator claim at
Yatala, the trial of Pole and the inquest on
Challerson, with their rendering of witnesses'
depositions in the manner of a newspaper
report, the riot at Green Valley and Oxley,
and the scene at the funeral of the agitator
Radetsky ? Yet, though these episodes are
given at great length, and do not form any
essential part of the story of Hereward Pole
and Ruth Allerton—the vindication of a
man's honour and the triumph of a woman's
invincible devotion—they are told with so
much intimate knowledge and strength of
colouring as almost to supply the absence of
a plot, and to make the story, apart from
artistic considerations, a really fine piece
of work.

It has a popularity in the English libraries
which is itself a proof of the service done by
the author to those who would know something of the careers of varying success and
bitter failure, of hardship and romantic
adventure, upon which so many of their
kinsmen set out forty years ago. *Nevermore*
and *The Sphinx of Eaglehawk* give other

views of the gold-digging days, chiefly of
their seamy side, but these stories offer
nothing that equals in interest the splendid
panorama of pioneer life revealed in *The
Miner's Right*.

Boldrewood has more than once insisted
with evident pleasure upon the general good
behaviour and manliness of the miners, and,
having been one of those all-seeing autocrats,
the gold-fields commissioners, he is an authority to be believed on the subject. In *Robbery
under Arms* the names are given of thirty
races represented on the Turon field, and
Hereward Pole, recounting his early impressions of Yatala, says: 'I was never done
wondering of what struck me as the chief
characteristic of this great army of adventurers suddenly gathered together from all
seas and lands, namely, its outward propriety
and submission to the law.' Elsewhere he
likens the sensible reticence which they observed respecting their own affairs and those
of their neighbours to the demeanour and
mode of thought which prevails in club life.

A passage from Dick Marston's account

of what he saw at Turon is worth reproducing
here as characteristic of the author's representation of a gold-fields community and as
a sample of his humour. The 'three
honourables,' of whom the disguised bushranger captain is one, are together in a
hotel.

'The last time I drank wine as good as this,' says
Starlight, 'was at the Caffy Troy, something or other, in
Paris. I wouldn't mind being there again, with the
Variety Opera to follow—would you, Clifford?'

'Well, I don't know,' says the other swell. 'I find this
amazing good fun for a bit. I never was in such grand
condition since I left Oxford. This eight hours' shift
business is just the right thing for training. I feel fit to
go for a man's life. Just feel this, Despard,' and he
holds out his arm to the camp swell. 'There's muscle
for you!'

'Plenty of muscle,' says Mr. Despard, looking round.
He was a swell that didn't work, and wouldn't work, and
thought it fine to treat the diggers like dogs. . . . 'Plenty
of muscle,' says he, 'but devilish little society.'

'I don't agree with you,' says the other honourable.
'It's the most amusing, and, in a way, instructive place
for a man who wants to know his fellow-creatures I was
ever in. I never pass a day without meeting some fresh
variety of the human race, man or woman; and their
experiences are well worth knowing, I can tell you. Not
that they're in a hurry to impart them; for that there's

more natural unaffected good manners on a digging than in any society I ever mingled in I shall never doubt. But when they see you don't want to patronise, and are content to be as simple man among men, there's nothing they won't do for you or tell you.'

'Oh, d——n one's fellow-creatures! present company excepted,' says Mr. Despard, filling his glass, 'and the man that grew this "tipple." They're useful to me now and then, and one has to put up with this crowd; but I never could take much interest in them.'

'All the worse for you, Despard,' says Clifford: 'you're wasting your chances—golden opportunities in every sense of the word. You'll never see such a spectacle as this, perhaps, again as long as you live. It's a fancy-dress ball with real characters.'

'Dashed bad characters, if we only knew,' says Despard, yawning. 'What do you say, Haughton?' looking at Starlight, who was playing with his glass, and not listening much, by the look of him.

In his latest novels Boldrewood reverts to his familiar themes. *The Sphinx of Eagle-hawk*, the shortest of all his works, might have been an excerpt from *The Miner's Right;* and the scene of *The Crooked Stick* is an inland station in New South Wales in the days of bushranging and disastrous droughts.

The materials employed in the latter story reproduce the principal features of almost a

score of other Australian novels published
within the last few years.   The love-affairs
of a beautiful, impulsive girl, sighing for
knowledge of the great world beyond the
limits of her narrow experience ; the influence upon her of a fascinating and gentlemanly Englishman, with aristocratic connections and a dubious past ; the manly young
Australian, whose loyalty, undervalued for a
time, is rewarded in the end—these are some
of the items which go to the making of a
class of story already somewhat too common.
The fact that Boldrewood continues to make
such subjects interesting is due largely to the
pervading sense of scrupulous truth, the evident element of personal experience, and the
general cheerfulness of tone, which are never
absent from any product of his pen, and
which constitute his highest claims to rank in
Australian literature.

MRS. CAMPBELL PRAED.

To Mrs. Campbell Praed belongs the credit
of being the first to attempt to give an extended and impartial view of the social and
political life of the upper classes in Australia.
While she has not ignored whatever seemed
picturesque in the external aspects of the
country, her chief concern has been with the
people themselves. Some of the best of her
works—*Policy and Passion* and *Miss Jacobsen's Chance*, for example—might fairly be
named as an answer to the somewhat common
complaint of a deficiency of dramatic suggestion in colonial life.

In a preface to the first-named novel, Mrs.
Praed explains it to have been her wish to
depict 'certain phases of Australian life, in
which the main interests and dominant

passions of the personages concerned are identical with those which might readily present themselves upon a European stage, but which directly and indirectly are influenced by striking natural surroundings and conditions of being inseparable from the youth of a vigorous and impulsive nation.'

The point of view here taken by the author at almost the beginning of her literary career has been maintained in most cases throughout her later work. The same preface might almost, in fact, serve for all her Australian stories. They describe broadly, in an attitude of good-natured criticism, the leading facts in the intellectual life of the people ; their proud self-reliance, tempered by an acute sense of isolation and its disadvantages ; their susceptibility to foreign criticism and example ; their frank, natural manners in social customs of native origin, contrasted with their quaintly-rigid observance of conventionalities which have long since been relaxed in the mother country whence they were copied.

Mrs. Praed has turned to account more

fully than any other writer the little affecta-
tions of that small upper crust of Antipodean
society which is sufficiently cultured to have
developed a taste for aristocratic European
habits, along with an uncomfortable suspicion
of 'bad form' in anything of purely local
growth. This is the class which maintains
an air of portentous solemnity in public
ceremonials, and is liable at any moment to
be convulsed by a question of precedence at
a Government House dinner.

From a lively appreciation of comedy to
caricature is an easy descent which the author
has not always resisted, but her exaggeration
is so obviously resorted to in the interests of
fun that it is unlikely to mislead. There is
certainly no need to repudiate as untypical of
Australian political society the Pickwickian
spectacle of a drunken Postmaster-General
fearfully trying to walk a plank after a Vice-
regal dinner, in order to win three dozen
of champagne wagered by the leader of the
Opposition, while the Premier looks on and
holds his sides with merriment ; or the case
of the Premier's wife, who, on being told by

a newly-arrived Governor—a musical enthu-
siast—that he hoped to be able to 'introduce
Wagner' at the local philharmonic concerts,
said : ' I'm sure we shall be very pleased to
see the gentleman.'

Considering, however, the opportunities
which colonial life, and especially colonial
politics, afford for ridicule, the author has
been commendably careful to avoid, as far as
possible, giving real offence. Yet her criticism is sufficiently free to be piquant, and, on
the whole, as salutary as it is entertaining.
'Why need Australians always be on the
defensive?' asks more than once an Englishman in one of her novels. The author seems
to have put the same question to herself as
an Australian, and to have decided that ultra-
sensitiveness is a worse vice than affectation,
and that her compatriots, by giving way to
it, do both themselves and their country an
injustice. For it implies a too low estimate
of what is fresh and strong and of real merit
in the independent life of the nation.

Colonists need a little more of the philosophic and common-sense spirit which can

look upon deficiencies and crudities merely
as phases in the natural evolution of society
in a new land.   This is what Mrs. Praed has
endeavoured to teach in some of her stories.
The lesson is often surrounded with a good
deal of bantering discussion ; it may not
always be apparent to an English reader,
but it can hardly be overlooked by an Australian.   There is rarely anything so pointed
as the conversation between Miss Jacobsen
and her lover, Chepstowe.   The former has
been wondering what the cultivated Englishman thought of a recent noisy and rather
vulgar reception tendered to a new Governor
for whom he is acting as private secretary.
Chepstowe is suspected of being secretly
amused at his surroundings.   But his view
of them is purely rational and matter-of-
fact.

' You know, I fancy you colonists think rather too
little of yourselves, and we in England rather too much.
Or I'll put it in another way.   I fancy you colonists
think too much about yourselves, and we in England
think too little.'

' You said just now that you think too much.'

' Yes ; it's the same thing put in a different way.   We

think too much of ourselves, and for that reason too little about ourselves. You are always thinking somebody is laughing at you ; we have made up our minds that we are the admiration of everybody. We are often very ridiculous, and don't know it. You often think you are ridiculous when you really are not.'

' I think we must have seemed very ridiculous the day you landed. . . . I know you are astonished at some of our public men. . . . You will write home and say how rude and rough and vulgar some of them are.'

' If one wants to see the ridiculous, one can see it everywhere. We have some public men at home who are rude and rough, and vulgar and ridiculous. . . . One has to make allowances, of course, for training and habits, and all that. . . . When our fellows are rough, there is less excuse for them. The more one goes about the world, the less one sees to laugh at, I think. . . .'

English self-complacency is, of course, a growth of centuries, but perhaps a deliberate and intelligent effort to acquire some of it in Australia would be the best specific for that consciousness which, colonists should not forget, is the mark of insignificance. It has been said that Australians already have too much to say for themselves and their country. The assertion is only applicable to a small boisterous class who have never seen anything beyond their own shores.

A much commoner element of Antipodean
life, one which some of Mrs. Praed's characters notably illustrate, is the desire for
wider experience and culture produced among
educated people by their constant use of
British and European literature.   James Ferguson, the young squatter in *The Head
Station*, represents those Australians who,
though stout believers in their own country,
feel its intellectual deficiencies—perhaps too
much ; who are more English than the
English themselves in their veneration for
the historic associations of the mother land ;
who, when they go to London, are curiously
at home in streets and among sights that
have been more or less definitely outlined in
their imagination from early childhood.

While three of his English-bred companions are exchanging reminiscences of
London life, Ferguson listens with an eager
interest, 'putting in a remark every now and
then which had the savour, so readily de-
tected, of acquaintance with the thing in
question by means of books rather than personal experience.'   In Mrs. Praed's stories,

as in real life, a personal acquaintance with other countries gives the Australian a truer appreciation of the good in his own. The man who has taken part in the artificialities of a London season, or has been a spectator of its petty rivalries, returns joyfully to a simpler life ; the woman who is prone to deify the smooth-spoken Englishman, learns through him to value the more homely virtues of colonial manhood.

In the difficult task of rendering attractive the restricted life of the squatting class, who form the country aristocracy of Australia, Mrs. Praed has combined humour and a terse cultivated style of expression with a dramatic sense, which has guided her past details that are merely commonplace. The natural surroundings of a head station furnish materials for bright little sketches immediately associated with some romantic episode in the story ; there is no vague straining to create 'atmosphere,' or anything that a judicious reader would skip.

The beautiful Honoria Longleat reclining in a hammock under the vine-trellised verandah

at Kooralbyn, stray shafts of sunlight impart-
ing a warm chestnut tint to her hair, a trail-
ing withe of orange begonia touching her
shoulder, a book in her lap and a bundle of
guavas on the ground beside her; Elsie
Valliant waiting for her lover on the rocky
crossing of Luya Dell, framed between two
giant cedars and outlined cameo-like against
the blue sky; Gretta Reay, the proud, sturdy
little belle of Doondi, with upturned sleeves
at her churn, pretending unconcern when she
is surprised by her English visitors—these
are some of the pictures in which the author
commemorates much that is noteworthy in
the warmth and colour of tropical Australia
and in the daily life of its inhabitants. This
fondness for posing her heroines is one of
the minor features of her work. Its results
in some of her later novels are not, however,
always agreeable : a few of the scenes in the
history of the unhappy Judith Fountain in
Affinities are painful, and the portrait, in *The
Brother of the Shadow*, of Mrs. Vascher as
she lies in the mesmerist's blue-silk-lined
room is an unnecessary ghastly elaboration.

The hardships suggested by the beginnings
of pastoral life amid the giant forests and
intense loneliness of Australia are never
allowed by Mrs. Praed to give a gloomy
colour to her stories.   It is one of their distinct merits that they present the humorous
incongruities rather than the trials of pioneer-
ing, though the latter are by no means
ignored.   In the first three chapters of *The
Romance of a Station* some excellent humour
is provided by the young bride's account of
her home-coming to the rude mansion on her
husband's mosquito-infested island station,
and the ludicrous privations she encountered
there.   There is nothing of the kind more
amusing in the whole of Australian fiction.
The description of the household pets, and
the vermin—including a lizard with an un-
canny habit of ' unfastening its tail and making
off on its stump when pursued '—rivals the
famous verandah scene in *Geoffry Hamlyn*.
An intimation in the preface that these
experiences are a faithful record from the
early life of the author herself sufficiently
explains their graphic quality.   Amusing also

are the sketches of the aristocratic settlers in *Policy and Passion* and *Outlaw and Law-maker* who try to apply the principles of æstheticism to the crude surroundings of their new-made homes in the backwoods—Dolph Bassett with his ornamental bridges and rockeries and his grand piano; Lord Horace Gage explaining with his maxim, ' If we can't be comfortable, let us at least be artistic,' a neglect to fill up the chinks in his slab hut.

Queensland, the scene of Mrs. Praed's colonial experience and the ' Leichardt's Land ' of her stories, differs notably from the rest of Australia only in climate; its social and political conditions are essentially the same in character as those in the rest of the country. The Englishman acquiring colonial experience, the squatter living in various stages of comfort or discomfort, the gentle-man spendthrift from whom his family has parted with the affectionate injunction, ' God bless you, dear boy; let us never see your face again!' and the political parties which go in and out of office ' like buckets in a

well ' (to use the author's own expression),
are, or have been, common features of every
colony.   Like several of her heroines, Mrs.
Praed alternated life in the country with the
gaieties of the capital.

The position of her father, the Hon. T. L.
Murray-Prior, as a member of the Legislative
Council, brought her into contact with those
political and vice-regal circles of which she
has given entertaining and occasionally
derisive accounts in *Policy and Passion*,
Miss Jacobsen's Chance, and elsewhere.   Her
description in the former story of the wealthy
landowners, who adopt a passive and somewhat disdainful attitude towards party strife,
applies to a class already large in the colonies.
Whether such an attitude is consistent with
' the truest conservatism to be found in Australia,' which they are said to represent, may
be questioned.   It seems rather to indicate
selfishness, petulance, and lack of patriotism.

It is not, however, upon the business of
politics or the humours and makeshifts of
colonial life that Mrs. Praed has expended
her best efforts as a writer.   Some study of

the human emotions is the primary interest
in all her novels. There is nearly always
love of the passionate and romantic kind,
prompted on the one side by impulse,
ignorance or glamour, and on the other by
passing fancy or self-interest : the love of an
innocent, unsophisticated woman for a man
experienced in the pleasures and some of
the darker vices of life ; and, in contrast, the
blunt respect and devotion of the typical
Australian man for the same woman, and her
light estimate of his worth. The tragedies
of marriage—the union of the refined and
imaginative with the coarse and commonplace, the high-souled with the worldly and
cynical, the pure with the impure—are
correlative themes of some of the strongest
of the novels. In these, pathos is the prevailing tone. We have the spectacle of the
woman's blind, illogical trust abused, her
helplessness in self-inflicted misery, or the
tenacity with which, in temptation, she clings
to the safeguards of conventional morality.
In most cases this tenacity, which the author
accounts an instinct rather than a virtue, is

either allowed to triumph, or is placed by
death beyond the possibility of a supreme
test. In the loves of Hester Murgatroyd
and Durnford in *The Head Station*, of Mrs.
Lomax and Leopold D'Acosta in *The Bond
of Wedlock*, and of Mrs. Borlase and Esmé
Colquhoun in *Affinities*, it is the woman who
directly, or by implication, insists upon
respect of the marriage tie so long as it
remains a legal obligation.

But it should be made clear that Mrs.
Praed is not in any sense a propagandist on
the subject of marriage. She illustrates,
often impressively, its difficulties and anomalies, but leaves the rest to the judgment of
the reader. The romantic, ignorant girl who
marries on trust, or is ready to do so, has
numerous representatives in these novels.
Though it is a woman's view of her trials
and unhappiness that is given, there is
nothing in the shape of a crusade against
male vices. It is not the faults of men that
are dwelt upon so much as the inevitably
lenient, the pitifully inadequate estimate
which women make of men themselves.

The most striking illustration of this
feature is probably contained in the last
scenes of *The Bond of Wedlock*, where the
heroine learns at once the hypocrisy of her
father and the dishonour of her lover. The
father, in a fit of resentment, has revealed the
mean plot by which she has been enabled to
divorce her husband and marry Sir Leopold
D'Acosta. The latter, seeing that Mrs.
Lomax would never consent to an elopement,
has paid another woman—a former mistress
of his—to incriminate Harvey Lomax, while
the audacious old humbug, his father-in-law,
does the business of a detective. Ariana's
dream of happiness is dissipated. She
hardens into indifference. The revelation
completes the disillusionment which had
already begun. 'I had set you up as my
hero, and my ideal, and I have found you—
a man.' This is the summary of her life's
experience, which in effect is also that of
Esther Hagart, Ginevra Rolt, Christina
Chard, Ina Gage, and others in the list of
Mrs. Praed's unhappy heroines. Married
life, as they illustrate it, is usually a com-

promise.   Even that of Mrs. Lomax is not
quite a failure.   Her husband does not
attempt to conceal the fact that she no longer
interests him, but with that commonly-
accepted philosophy which recognises a wife
as at least an adjunct to conventional respectability, he reminds her that, after all,
their union has some advantages :

> 'I would much rather have you for a wife than any
> other woman I ever knew ; and if I sometimes think a
> man is better who hasn't a wife, it is only when you are
> in one of those reproachful moods, and seem as if you
> were anxious to make me out a heartless sort of mis-
> creant.   In Heaven's name, why not make the best of
> things?   Why need we be melodramatic?   We are man
> and woman of the world.   We must take the world as we
> find it, and ourselves for what it has made us.'

Ariana's answer was given later on when
she realized the full extent to which she had
been self-deluded : 'I am not going to be
melodramatic.   We can be very good friends
on the outside.   We need never be anything
more.'

A strong bias towards analysis is the chief
characteristic of Mrs. Praed's studies in char-

acter. As in her illustrations of the per-
plexing uncertainties of married life it is the
woman's point of view that is most impressively presented, so in each story there is at
least one woman whose personality stands
out in pathetic relief and claims paramount
attention. She is usually a cultivated woman
of romantic tendency, living in a restricted
social environment, and displaying the craving
of that class of her sex for change, pleasurable excitement, and sympathy. In the
satisfaction of her yearnings or ambitions
are seen, perhaps more often than is typical,
the gloomy aspects of marriage, and the in-
competence of women to manage their own
lives.

The average Australian girl of real life is
neither very romantic nor fastidious. She is
cheerful, adaptable, too fond of pleasure to
be thoughtful, and has a decided inclination
towards married life. Its material advantages
and status attract her—and, for the rest, she
has a vague confidence that everything will
come right. Nowhere is the horror of elderly
spinsterhood more potent. The influence of

independent professional life fostered by the large public schools is still infinitesimal.

The type upon which Mrs. Praed has bestowed her most elaborate work belongs to a class both higher and far fewer in numbers. It is the class that Mr. Froude had chiefly in view when he noted the absence of 'severe intellectual interests' as a deficiency of society at Sydney.

Honoria Longleat, the principal study of Mrs. Praed's second novel, may, with a few obvious deductions, be taken as a fair example of the colonial woman educated beyond sympathy with her native surroundings, and unprovided with any employment for her mental energies. With the distractions and interests of her narrow circle exhausted, and the knowledge that her future—her only possible future—must soon be decided by marriage, she is consumed with an intense and reckless desire for new emotional experience. Her unrest is like that of the large class of American women who are educated above the purely commercial standard of their fathers and brothers, and are impelled to satisfy their intellectual cravings by frequent European travel.

'This is only a state of half-existence,' said Honoria in reference to her country life in Australia. 'Books are so unsatisfying! I read them greedily at first, then throw them aside in disgust. They never take one below the surface . . . I want to grow and live. . . . What is the use of living unless one can gauge one's capacity for sensation?' Gretta Reay, in whom the same discontent is reproduced, exclaims: 'Ah, we Australians are like birds shut up in a large cage—our lives are little and narrow, for all that our home is so big.'

By these and other characters of the same type, the cultivated Englishman, who offers them the prospect of change and emancipation from monotony, is distinctly preferred in marriage to the man of colonial birth and experience. 'Don't you know,' says Gretta to one of the latter, 'that an Australian girl's first aim is to captivate an Englishman of rank and be translated to a higher sphere—failing that, to make the best of a rich squatter?'

The heroine of *Outlaw and Lawmaker* differs from Gretta only in being more emphatic in her preference for the doubtful stranger, and irrational in her objections to her tried Australian lover, Frank Hallett. Once, in a riding-party, 'she had moodily watched his (Hallett's) square, determined bushman's back as he jogged along in front of her, and compared it with Blake's easy, graceful, rather rakish, bearing. Why was Frank so stolid, so good, so commonplace?'

A trifling superficial defect of the same sort turns the tables against the gallant young explorer, Dyson Maddox, in his first suit for the hand of Miss Longleat. The half-dozen analytical studies of female character in the principal novels of Mrs. Praed are far from flattering to her countrywomen, and might be somewhat misleading if we permitted ourselves to forget that in every case it is only one phase of a colonial girl's life that is being given.

The whims, the countless flirtations, the greed for new sensations, the inconsistencies and the apparent mercenary attitude towards

marriage, are not more permanently characteristic of the women of Australia than of
Englishwomen with equal opportunities. The
impulses of the former are under few conventional restraints ; they have a greater control
of their lives : that is the only material difference. The matrimonial creed of Gretta
Reay expresses rather the exaggerated
cynicism of a coquette than a fact generally
true of the class to which she belongs. The
experiences of herself and of other leading
characters in these stories correctly show
that, although Australian women have an
undoubted preference for the gentlemanly
product of an older civilisation, it is a preference of sentiment in which self-interest
and prudence are scarcely considered.

Even Weeta Wilson, the professional
beauty so strikingly portrayed in *The
Romance of a Station*, has a soul above her
own avowed commercial view of marriage.
It had been systematically planned that she
should contract an aristocratic alliance ; for
years she had co-operated with her parents
in elaborate preparations, half pathetic, half

ludicrous ; she had been guarded and nur-
tured like a hothouse-plant. At last, when
her opportunity came, she relinquished her
lover on finding that there was another who
had a prior right to him.

The subtle skill with which some of the
nobler qualities of her women are brought
out, especially their capacity for self-sacrifice
and devotion, marks Mrs. Praed's highest
point of achievement in the portrayal of
character. Her knowledge of the mental
complexities of her own sex is both deeper
and better expressed than her observation of
men. In the most inconsistent, the most
cynical, or the shallowest of her women, there
is a latent tenderness, a soft womanliness,
which conquers dislike. Thus, it is impossible
to lack sympathy for Christina Chard, or
accept her own estimate of her selfishness,
after reading the finely-written scene in which
she is found kneeling by the bedside of
her dying child, from whom she has been so
cruelly separated, while her recreant husband
stands apart in awe and humiliation ; or,
again, in the interview with Frederica Bar-

nadine, when the claims of both women to the love of Rolf Luard are discussed.

The absence of similar redeeming qualities in several of the principal male characters leaves them almost wholly without definite claim on our regard, and also lessens the effect of the author's frequent endeavours to impartially contrast the unconsciously low moral standard of the average worldly man —the standard which society accepts—with the high, impracticable ideals of inexperienced womanhood.

The heroines in nearly all of Mrs. Praed's stories have the life of sentiment and passion revealed to them by men older in years, and skilled in those small arts and graces of refined society which are ever attractive to women. But, in fulfilling this design, the men themselves are often placed in a strained and artificial pose. The presentation of the purely emotional side of their nature inevitably tends to produce an appearance of weakness and effeminacy.

There is hardly a single admirable quality in Barrington, the base lover of Honoria

Longleat; or in George Brand, who deserts
Esther Hagart in her poverty and loneliness,
and years afterwards, on finding her recognised as the niece of an English baronet,
persuades her into an unhappy marriage; or
in Brian Gilmore, the profligate in *Moloch*,
who seeks to rejuvenate his jaded passions
with the love of an innocent girl, after abandoning another woman whose life he has
spoiled. Sir Bruce Carr-Gambier forsakes
Christina Chard and her child for cowardly
reasons similar to those pleaded by Brand.
When they meet, long after, he offers his
devotion again, but only because her developed beauty, position, and reputed wealth
attract him.

It is true that these characters fairly fulfil
the author's intention, so far as they bring
into vivid juxtaposition the polished life of
the old world with the simplicity of the new,
and help to give the necessary dramatic
point to the several stories; but there is so
much of the cad in their nature and conduct,
that it is difficult to accept them as representatives of any conceivable type of the

Englishman of birth and refinement. This
result, however, does not imply any actual
inability on the part of the author to realise
the standard of true manhood in all its varying strength and foibles, its tenderness and
honour. Where there has not seemed any
necessity to bend the character to the re-
quirements of the story, admirably life-like
sketches of men have been produced—such
as Rolf Luard in *Christina Chard* and
Bernard Comyn in *An Australian Heroine*
among Englishmen; and Dyson Maddox,
Frank Hallett, and James Ferguson among
Australians.

Though it is plain that Mrs. Praed has
generally found colonial men wanting in interest in proportion as they themselves lack
the polish that travel and extended experience of social life impart, she has not overlooked the rugged dignity, the truth and
virility, which are their highest characteristics. Alluding to Ferguson as one type
of his country, she observes that, 'underlying the rough-and-ready manners and the
prosaic routine of bush-life, there is an old-

world chivalry, a reverence for women, a
purity of thought, a delicacy of sentiment.
. . . This is partly due to the breezy moral
atmosphere, and partly to the influence of
books, which become living realities in the
solitude and monotony of existence among
the gum-trees. The typical Australian is
an odd combination of the practical and the
ideal. He is a student who learns to read
to himself a foreign language, but does not
attain to its pronunciation. He has no
knowledge of the current jargon or society
slang. He has unconsciously rejected vulgar-
isms and shallow conceits ; but all the deeper
thoughts, the poetry of life, which appeal to
the soul, he has made his own.'

Ferguson himself echoes the same estimate
in pleading his suit with Miss Reay. 'It
seems to me,' he says, 'that there's a kind
of chivalry which can be practised in the
bush here better than in great cities—the
chivalry Tennyson writes about—the knighthood that isn't earned by sauntering through
life in a graceful, smiling sort of way, with
your heart in your hand, but in simplicity

and faith ; by love of one woman, and reverence of all women for her sake.'

Compared with the fascinating aristocrats
and adventurers, the Australian man seems
crudely provincial. Yet he is never shown
in an incorrect or merely satirical light.
There are, to be sure, occasions when he
appears too tame and Dobbin-like in acceptance of his lady's caprices ; but this is partly
an evidence of that mixture of stiff native
pride and independence which forbids servile
appeal even to one he loves.

The deficiency of which the reader is most
often conscious in endeavouring to make a
general estimate of Mrs. Praed's work is a
want of breadth in her scope—a presentation
too constant and too tense of certain phases
of the passionate life of men and women, to
the comparative exclusion of those softer and
higher attributes which even Charlotte Brontë
(whose touch that of Mrs. Praed occasionally
resembles) did not neglect. In other words,
we are not given enough to admire. There
are few pictures—and none that can be called
memorable—of happy married life to contrast

with the vivid tragedies of mistaken unions.
An inclination towards humorous disdain
characterizes the references in the stories
to conjugal relations of the ordinarily satis-
factory kind. And when those of a filial
nature are brought into prominence, they, too,
often have only a pathetic or painful aspect
—love on the one side repelled by indifference ; an uncouth parent offering rough sympathy that irritates instead of soothes ; a
sensitive girl writhing under the brutalities
or *gaucheries* of a drunken father.

A survey of the author's female characters
will recall over a score of names of discontented girls experimenting in life—flirts,
minxes, unhappy wives, and shallow society
women ; while after passing over half a dozen
of the *ingénue*, the amusing and the neutral
types, there remain only about four to represent the highest and most lovable qualities
of womanhood. A similar division might be
made between the male characters, though
here the preponderance of the bad would
not be so great as in the first case.

The descriptions of English society which

are amongst Mrs. Praed's best work are marked by the same clear vision of the darker side of human nature that is displayed in the treatment of English character in her Australian novels. Her view of the 'smart' section of English society is somewhat severe. After reading several of her novels, one could almost imagine her defending her literary preference in the words of Esmé Colquhoun, in *Affinities:* 'What is our mission—we writers—but to distil the essence of the age? The critics tell us that we are complex, that we are corrupt, that we are anatomists of diseased minds. We reply: The age is complex; the age is corrupt, and the society we depict is the outcome of influences which have been gathering through centuries of advancing civilization . . . the reign of healthy melodrama is over; the reign of analysis has commenced. We make dramas of our sensations, not of our actions.' The same view is expressed in an article contributed by Mrs. Praed to the *North American Review* in 1890. 'Analysis, not action,' she notes as the prevailing characteristic of the fiction

17

produced by female writers, 'as it is also of our modern social life.' But, 'to dissect human nature under its society swathings needs,' she adds, 'the skill of a Balzac or a Thackeray, while the feminine counterpart of a Balzac or a Thackeray is difficult to find.'

That indefinable power which includes sympathetic insight and does not overlook whatever is good even in the most repulsive character is, perhaps, what the describers in fiction of modern society need even more than skill in dissection. To observe and dissect what is corrupt is easier than to make the record of corruption presentable. Mrs. Praed's own tale *The Bond of Wedlock*, with all its undoubted cleverness, its realism and dramatic strength, fails in its due impression as a picture of latter-day English morals because it is too sordid, too completely devoid of any of the better qualities of humanity.

To see Mrs. Praed in her most agreeable and natural moods one must revert to the novels in which the scenery and people of her own country are described. In *Miss Jacobsen's Chance* we have her liveliest example of humour and caricature, in *The Head Station* her most cheerful pictures of country life, and in *Christina Chard* some account of the society with which colonists of wealth surround themselves in London. The latter story has several finely dramatic scenes and is a sample of the author's mature work. Hers is the most comprehensive view that we have of the social and political life of the Antipodes, and for this and for her minutely recorded knowledge of her own sex she will long continue to hold and deserve a foremost place in Australian literature.

TASMA.

BETWEEN the writers who profess not to
see anything individual in the life of Australia and those others who confine themselves to describing a few of its principal
scenes and types of character, Tasma holds a
middle and independent place. She is absolutely without predilections and hobbies. Her
materials are chosen for some quality of
picturesqueness rather than for the purpose
of illustrating any phase of life at the Antipodes or elsewhere. So little are some of
her novels concerned with the external ap-
pearances of the country that the scene of
their action might easily be transferred to
almost any part of Great Britain or America.
 Incidentally she has given a few strongly-
sketched views of places—of Melbourne in

midsummer, with its buildings of sombre
bluestone and stucco, and streets swept by
dust-laden hot winds ; of Riverina, arid and
drought-stricken ; and of the peaceful beauty
of rural Tasmania, the home of her own
youth—but these and other descriptions from
the same pen are slight compared with
similar work in the stories of Kingsley,
Boldrewood, and Mrs. Campbell Praed.

Tasma, as one of the younger writers, has
rightly seen that, for the present at all events,
more than sufficient use has been made in
fiction of the natural peculiarities of Australia. Her novels are, moreover, all character studies, and little dependent upon local
colour for their interest. Her quiet, satirical
humour and power of rapidly and mordantly
sketching a portrait, do much to justify a
comparison which her friends sometimes
make of her writings with those of George
Eliot and Jane Austen. Rolf Boldrewood,
after the publication of her first three books,
hailed her as the ' Australian George Eliot,'
and the title is certainly more fitting than the
praise implied by the other comparison. She

has much of George Eliot's conscientious literary expression, direct masculine way of looking at life, and unsparing criticism of her own sex. While reminding one, as she often does, of Jane Austen's humour, Tasma does not approach any nearer to that writer's supreme gift of describing character in dialogue than scores of others who have followed the same model during the last seventy years.

Like most of the chief contributors to Australian literature, Tasma is a colonist in experience only. She was born at Highgate, near London, and taken during childhood by her father, Mr. Alfred James Huybers, a Dutch merchant, to Hobart, in Tasmania, about forty years ago. She displayed literary talent at an early age, read extensively, and published criticisms in the *Melbourne Review*, and short stories and sketches in the lighter colonial periodicals.

In 1879 Tasma went to live in Europe, and has since known Australia only as an occasional visitor. Becoming interested in social questions during a residence in France, she wrote in the *Nouvelle Revue*, suggesting emigration to the colonies and engagement in the fruit-growing industry there as a means of relieving some of the poverty of the Old World. She afterwards lectured on the subject in French at the invitation of the Geographical Society of Paris. So successful were the lectures that she was induced to repeat them in various provincial centres, as well as in Holland and Belgium. This work occupied from 1880 to 1882, and Tasma was presented by the French Government with the decoration of Officier d'Académie. The King of the Belgians also honoured the lecturer by receiving her in special audience to discuss means of improving communication between Belgium and Tasmania.

In 1885, after revisiting Australia, Tasma was married to M. Auguste Couvreur, a distinguished Belgian politician and journalist (he has since died), and four years later began her career as a novelist by the publication at London of *Uncle Piper of Piper's Hill,* which proved to be one of the most notable books of its season.

This novel remains the best example of

the author's humour and power of describing character that she has produced. It has none of the marks of a first effort. Written when Tasma was about thirty-two, it embodied some of the best fruits of many years' keenly critical study of life, in addition to the culture gained by travel and a wide course of reading. Of plot there is little—there is still less in some of the later novels—but sufficient variety of incident is given to afford scope for unusually rich faculties of sympathy and philosophic observation.

In her desire to present only real persons moving in a familiar world she merits, in *Uncle Piper*, praise almost equal to that accorded by Nathaniel Hawthorne to the novels of Anthony Trollope when he spoke of them as being 'as real as if some giant had hewn a great lump out of the earth and put it under a glass case, with all its inhabitants going about their daily business and not suspecting that they were being made a show of.' It is, however, less of Trollope than of Howells that Tasma reminds the reader in this first story. The character of the wealthy *parvenu* uncle, sensitive, boastful, resentful, and obstinate, yet tender-hearted as a child, irresistibly recalls *Silas Lapham*, that wonderfully natural and sympathetic presentment of a commonplace man. There are numerous points of resemblance between the two, especially when they are shown contrasted with their aristocratic friends. The delightful comradeship of Lapham and his wife, with its curiously dry New England expression, has its counterpart in Piper's affection for his sister and their pride in each other.

The half-acknowledged social ambitions of both men, qualified by their secret contempt for the pretensions of the upper classes, is shown in various similar ways, as is also their love of display. They differ only as their nationalities differ. Puritanism survives in the American merchant and his wife, and unconsciously sways their lives. Uncle Piper's conception of the Deity is of the vaguest kind, but he has a religion of generosity and love which in the end nothing can repress—which survives the effects of a temper soured by systematic coldness and opposition on the part of a rebellious son and step-daughter. While in his relations with his womenkind—the tractable section of them — there is nothing of that quaint American delicacy and reserve noted by Howells, there is in its stead an absorbing tenderness which is irresistible.

The superiority of Silas Lapham as a realistic portrait is not difficult to affirm ; still, it is a fact complimentary to Tasma that the characters thus far approximate. Uncle Piper is under all the disadvantage that a figure in fiction suffers in being described largely in plain statement by the author instead of being gradually revealed in piquant dialogue.

Readers of *Silas Lapham* will remember the rapid series of witty touches with which the burly Bostonian is sketched as he sits in the office of his warehouse, surrounded by samples of the mineral paint that he is so pathetically proud of, striving to maintain a dignified indifference as he answers the rather flippant curiosity of the local press interviewer. Uncle Piper, on the other hand, is introduced, as all of Tasma's characters are, in sundry solid-looking pages of direct narrative. It is true that their humour and epigram make bright reading, but they are necessarily without the power of pithy dialogue to create a vivid impression of character.

Whether Uncle Piper is a type of Australian plutocracy need hardly be discussed. Of plebeian tradesmen grown wealthy every community has its proportion. It may, however, be said that the owners of luxurious villas in the suburbs of Melbourne have individually a good deal more grammar and less generosity than he who was described by one of his fashionable English guests as possessing 'the home of a West-End magnate and the intonation of a groom.' The author herself would probably disclaim any intention to represent a type. She is one of those writers who doubt the existence of types in the ordinary meaning of the term, and she certainly makes no conscious attempt to delineate them.

A passage in her third novel, *The Penance*

of Portia James, gives her views on this subject, and incidentally upon Australian character. A description is furnished of a breakfast-party in the London home of an Australian who has made his fortune in a silver-mine, and from being a *habitué* of colonial racecourses has lately developed into a patron of art and a purchaser of dubious 'old masters' at exorbitant prices.

To hold up the assembled party to the eyes of English readers as thoroughly typical Australians would be as unjust a proceeding as was that of Dumas *père* when he declared that all the inhabitants of Antwerp were *roux* because he had encountered two red-headed girls on his way to the hotel. No one is thoroughly typical unless he be a savage or a peasant. Portia and her relatives retained their own underlying individualities none the less that they had been influenced in their outward bearing and modes of expressing themselves by a long sojourn in the backwoods of Victoria, in daily contact with all sorts and conditions of men—broken-down gentlemen, English yokels, bush-hands, and the like. After all, the moulding of character by outward influences alone is not a work to be achieved in one generation, or what would become of the theory of heredity, upon which everything is supposed to depend, more or less, in our present scientific age? If these people strike the English reader, therefore, as differing in certain respects from those he is accustomed to meet in his daily walk through life, let him remember that the

differences which will strike him most are the merely
superficial ones resulting from an occasional departure
from the conventional rules of speech and behaviour that
guide his own outward conduct, and that in all the main
essentials they are, *au fond*, neither more like him or
more unlike him than though chance had willed that
they should be born and brought up on the selfsame
patch of earth as himself. A difference in the vocabulary of the native-born Australian, or long resident in
Australia, of the not too highly educated order, as well
as a difference in his tone of voice and enunciation, from
that of a person belonging to a corresponding class in
England, is one of those facts, however, which 'nobody
can deny.' I am not going to enter in this connection
upon a disquisition respecting the relative merits of what
Mrs. James would have called 'höfisch' English, and
the English that has been coined out of entirely new
conditions by pioneers and backwoodsmen. Suffice it
to say there *is* a difference, and Portia was never more
sensible of it than when she returned, as on the present
occasion, from moving among a London society crowd
into the Anglo-Australian social atmosphere of the Kensington house.

Tasma's efforts to give variety to her work,
and keep as far as possible out of the beaten
paths of the Australian writer, have not, however, quite excluded from her novels characters which will be recognised as typical.
There is, for instance, the young pleasure-

loving colonial man who keeps racehorses, gets deeply into debt and love, and has sometimes to encounter awkward parental alternatives.

At least three excellent portraits of such men are given. The best is that of George Drafton, in *In Her Earliest Youth*. In no other novel are the rough good-nature and loose, slangy talk of the young Australian sportsman of the upper-middle class more naturally expressed. The author's knowledge of the cant terms and short cuts in the vocabulary of the not necessarily ill-educated but supremely careless colonial young man is almost equal to that of Rolf Boldrewood, who has been listening to the talk of such men all his life.

Uncle Piper's exasperating 'gentleman' son George is also a noticeably clever creation in a book full of good portraits; and it is a tribute to the author's skill that as the story progresses our sympathy for him increases rather than diminishes, notwithstanding the needless agonies of rage he occasions his father.

The most vivid chapter to be found in any of Tasma's novels is that in which Uncle Piper, after witnessing a love-scene between Laura Lydiat and George, sends for the latter and threatens to cast him off if a marriage of the pair should take place. Laura is an agnostic and a sort of 'new woman' who maintains a constant attitude of disdain towards her stepfather. She and George have spent much of their youth together, discussed pessimistic theories in Piper's hearing, and generally ignored him, and made him feel his ignorance in ways very trying to the temper of a man who, 'now that his money-making days were over, had a passion for dictating absolutely to everyone about him.' 'He'd talk' and 'she'd talk,' as Mr. Piper would complain; 'and they'd spout their scraps of poetry that hadn't an ounce of the sense any good, honest old rhyme could show; and you'd think, to hear them, they were doing their Maker a favour by condescending to go on living at all!'

An alliance of this kind between the two people for whom he had done most with his wealth was bad enough, but Uncle Piper was determined that it should not become a closer one. Was this not one reason for his importation of an entire family of impoverished relatives, that they and his little pet daughter, the angelic Louey, should readjust the balance of household power in his favour?

It was on the eve of the arrival of his aristocratic connections, the Cavendishes, that he determined to put a stop to his son's courtship. George, at the outset of the momentous interview with his father, speculated inwardly on his chances of being able to soften the old man to a favourable view of 'the only wish that he had ever framed with a feeling that savoured of intensity.'

Before entering the ornamental tower where his father awaited him, George had composed his face to its usual expression of laziest indifference. His imperturbability always 'had the effect of a goad upon his father's temper. His face never changed colour when the old man's was purple. His voice never lost its measured drawl.'

As Mr. Piper turned and faced him you would never

have traced the sonship in George. There was nothing in common between the sallow, indolent face of the younger man, and the spreading, heated face of the elder. George looked like any club-lounger—not un-willing to let it be seen that he is slightly bored, yet ready, with perfect acquiescence, to go through with an hour or a forenoon of the infliction of boredom, as con-veyed by a father's presence. . . . Mr. Piper watched him as he continued tranquilly to pare his nails, the baffled sense of helplessness that exasperated him at the outset of an interview with his son creeping over him as he watched. If George could only once have lost his head and sworn, or only once implored or threatened! But he never did. The apathy and unconcern of his attitude—the veiled disrespect it implied—spoke of an indifference that was worse than the most open revolt. But surely he would be made to feel now! Mr. Piper had never tried to reach 'my gentleman' through his 'young woman' yet. . . . A slight elevation of an un-ruffled brow just gave evidence that though his eyes were looking critically at his almond-shaped finger-nails, his ear took in the sense of his father's words. Otherwise he might have served as a perfect model of intentness upon his hands, as the statue of the boy who to all eternity will be absorbed in the task of extracting a thorn from his foot.

Meanwhile Mr. Piper is in a state of acute excitement.

'I'll see and put a stop to it!' he threatened. 'I'll take and pack her off, and you at the back of her, "my gentleman"!' George knew that the use of this expres-

sion signified especial bitterness on his father's part.
' I'll have an end of this nonsense—a painted jade like
her !'

' Wait a minute, please,' said George, shutting the
knife with a little snap, and settling himself back upon
the window-sill ; 'you are a little hard to follow, or I am
slow at catching your meaning, perhaps. I understand
that you had some object in sending for me. Are you
explaining it to me now? I am quite prepared to listen,
as you see.'

' You're very condescending, I'm sure,' said Mr. Piper,
with such withering sarcasm that George stroked his
moustache and smiled. ' You put yourself about for
your father a deal too much, " my gentleman," there's
no doubt of it.' Then, with a sudden break in his
voice : ' No, George ; it's not much of a son you've been
to me, and no one can say I've stood in your light. I'd
like you to show me another young man who could carry
on top ropes like you. There's not many fathers 'ud
have stood it. Most fathers 'ud made you turn to long
ago.'

' Do you want anything done for you?' interrupted
George, with the air of a man who is laying himself out
to oblige—' another tour of inspection in the north ?'

Whenever Mr. Piper made allusion to George's want
of occupation, it was the young man's policy to refer to
this tour of inspection—a memorable tour, seeing that it
had given him employment for at least three months. . . .

If there was anything humiliating in being rated as an
' able-bodied young man who wasn't worth his salt,' as a
loafer who was hardly fit to 'jackaroo' on a station, as
a ' lazy lubber ' who would ' go to the dogs if it weren't

for his father,' George never betrayed that he felt humiliated by so much as the twitching of an eyelid. Persistently stroking the ends of his moustache with an air of profound abstraction, he made it apparent, as soon as Mr. Piper stopped to take breath, that he was suppressing an inclination to yawn.

'I dare say it's all very true, governor,' was all he said in reply. 'It's very nice and complimentary, I'm sure, and I ought to be very much obliged to you. But, *à propos* of your compliments, may I ask if it was only to treat me to them in full that you brought me up those confounded tower steps this morning? Because, in that case, I wouldn't have minded waiting, you know. It's hardly fair upon a man, is it, to put him to the treadmill before he's well awake in the morning?'

'If you were like other young men,' retorted Mr. Piper, 'you'd be up and down them steps twenty times a day' (George shuddered); 'but oh no! my gentleman can crawl on to the lawn and carry on with a——'

'Stop there!' cried George, in a tone that made his father silent through sheer astonishment (George had never been known to raise his voice before). 'Do you know the relation in which Laura stands to me?'

He looked Mr. Piper full in the face as he said it, and seeing the ghastly change that came over the face as he looked, he felt that he had been over-hasty. For the glass through which Mr. Piper had made a feint of looking dropped from his quivering fingers and his lips worked in a distorted fashion over his discoloured teeth; the blood rushing away from his florid cheeks left them streaked with thready, sanguineous veins, mottling the ash-coloured patches; and rushed back again with a force that seemed to swell the veins round his temples to bursting. . . .

'What's the matter, father?' said George at last, not with any of Louey's vehement alarm, but eyeing him rather gravely and curiously. 'Do you object to my looking upon Laura in the light of a—*sister?*'

'Eh?' said Mr. Piper. His power of articulation was slowly returning, but his breath as yet was only equal to the monosyllable.

'Of a sister,' repeated George slowly, 'and a friend.'

'Your *sister!*' said Mr. Piper, as soon as he could speak distinctly. 'That's as you choose to take it. She's none o' mine, thank God! But you take and make her more than your sister, and see how soon you'll come to repent it. It's down in my will. I've sworn it. Dead or alive, I won't have the jade in my family! If you've got a fancy for her, you may take her, but never come anigh Piper's Hill again!'

'You mistake the position of affairs,' said George calmly. 'Laura wouldn't have me if I wanted!'

'Ho, ho!' Mr. Piper's laugh was more insulting than mirthful. 'That's why she comes and hugs you on the lawn of a morning, is it?'

The interview ended with an intimation that Mr. Piper will not have Laura as a daughter-in-law 'at any price,' and that if George choose to marry her it must be as a pauper, and unrelieved of his heavy burden of turf debts. Piper's stormy, almost speechless anger, like his craving for sympathy and approval, are alike often exceedingly pathetic. His personality, though less delicately drawn than that of his niece, Sara Cavendish, is a striking figure throughout the book. A good delineation of an old man is sufficiently rare in fiction to make that of Uncle Piper notable. Tasma has not equalled this performance in any of her other works. Josiah Carp, the Melbourne merchant in *In Her Earliest Youth*, and Sir Matthew Bogg, another of the same class, in the short story *Monsieur Caloche*, are shown only in a satirical and repulsive light, which necessarily makes them appear somewhat unreal.

As a vivid study, combined with excellent comedy, the portrait of Sara Cavendish would not have been unworthy of Thackeray. The selfishness concealed by her demure exterior and great beauty, and the absurdly excessive estimate of her virtues made by the Reverend Francis Lydiat, are a warning to all susceptible young men. Lydiat was a passenger by the ship which carried Sara and her parents to Australia. When he

gave his weekly sermons during the voyage,
Miss Cavendish was always present, and
looked at him with her large eyes to such
purpose that they 'seemed to be absorbing
his meaning into the soul of their pos-
sessor.'

But there was nothing ethereal in Sara's
thoughts. 'She had a fancy for imagining
becoming dresses. She would build up a
delightful wardrobe in the air, entering into
as many details of her airy outfit as though it
could be instantly materialised. And she
liked to imagine a becoming background for
her own beautiful person, in which a husband
with the essentials of good birth and un-
limited money, and the desirable qualifications of an air of distinction and great
devotion to her, filled a reasonable space.'
Lydiat had often seen her lost in daydreams
such as it would have seemed to him almost
a sacrilege to disturb, 'though it is probable
that the only notion he would have been
guilty of upsetting had reference to the
shape of an imaginary velvet train.'

The insight and completeness with which

Sara's character is depicted in the course of the story make it impossible that the reader should entirely dislike her as a mere sample of the calculating coquette. She is one of that large class of women, with a limited capacity for affection, whose natures expand only in an atmosphere of luxury. ' Don't be shocked,' she says to her sister in reference to the unsuccessful suit of her clerical lover ; ' I never intended to be a poor man's wife.' As a contrast to the cold personality of the beautiful Sara, the author gives a charming picture of the elder sister's affection and thoughtfulness for others.

Margaret Cavendish and Eila Frost, in *Not Counting the Cost*, are good women of a perfectly possible and natural kind, and it is surprising to think that the same hand which drew them also found patience to draw the unhappy, metaphysical heroines of *In Her Earliest Youth* and *The Knight of the White Feather*. Tasma is seldom so pleasing as when describing the characters of children, of whom several figure prominently in her novels. There is a delightful picture of romping childhood at the opening of *Not Counting the Cost.* The scene is a farm in the shadow of Mount Wellington, near Hobart, the city where the author spent many of her own early years. 'Chubby,' the eight-year-old uncle of the heroine of *In Her Earliest Youth*, and Louey Piper are lovable creations, though, it must be said, more quaint than natural. One remembers the expansive dignity of the former on his first meeting with Pauline's lover, George Drafton. 'How do you do, little man?' says the latter condescendingly. 'How do you do, sir?' replies the little man stiffly, raising his garden hat. 'You are an acquaintance of Paul—of Miss Vyner's, I believe. I have the honour to be her maternal uncle.' No wonder George bursts into a loud guffaw, notwithstanding the tragic intensity of his love protestations of five minutes before!

Louey Piper's relations with her father are idyllic. She is more necessary to him than Eppie to Silas Marner; she is a continual negotiator of peace in his divided house, and 'in this she could not have displayed more courtier-like sagacity had she been an old-world changeling with centuries of experience respecting rich fathers of uncertain testamentary inclinations.' In her limited knowledge of things outside Piper's Hill, 'street-crossings and railway-platforms presented themselves to her in the light of shocking and mysterious man-traps. . . . The wistful, yearning look that gave her eyes so touching an expression in the setting of her small freckled face never gave place to such a fulness of satisfaction as when her father, her brother, and her sister were all, as it were, under her eye, and safe to remain indoors for the night.'

The general praise won by *Uncle Piper* for its author as a delineator of character appears to have decided her to give increased attention to her ability in this direction. The immediate result was scarcely a happy one. The analytical bias disclosed in the first story was largely extended in the second, with the usual accompaniment of a decrease in action and humour. Pauline Vyner, the central

figure of *In Her Earliest Youth*, a sensitive
and speculative girl, marries without love a
man who has saved the life of a child to
whom she is much attached. In tastes and
intellectual bent the pair are almost without
anything in common. The story—an unusually long three-volume one—is mainly a
minute study of Pauline's disillusionment
during the early period of her wifehood :
how she escaped the temptations placed in
her way by a man who had formerly attracted
her ; and how, with the birth of her first child,
she experienced the dawn of affection for its
father.

The story is excessively expanded for the
small amount of dramatic movement it contains. Only three characters are prominently
described, and these too seldom through the
medium of dialogue. The central motive,
moreover, is lacking in strength. It is difficult to appreciate the tragic pathos of so
common a matrimonial error as Pauline's,
especially as George, though uncongenial in
his tastes, and not exempt from the ordinary
weaknesses of men, is entirely devoted to

her, and would readily have improved under her influence, had she chosen to exert any. Tasma's more recent work is better both in spirit and literary construction. Very sympathetic and entertaining is the narrative, in *Not Counting the Cost*, of the adventures of the Clare family in their quixotic travels in search of the cousin who is to restore them a long-lost heritage. In this story and *The Penance of Portia James* the author gives some interesting scenes of Paris life. But to get the best samples of her humour, one must return to her first novel. The burlesque of Piper's pompous, genteel brother-in-law is delicious. Mr. Cavendish affects to be revolted by the necessity of being indebted to the *ci-devant* butcher, while secretly luxuriating in his munificence. Finally, as a means of discharging some of his obligations, he conceives the project of hunting up a pedigree for his plebeian relative, after the manner of the enterprising person who opened a 'heraldry office' in Sydney about fifty years ago, and announced his readiness to provide clients with reliable information of

their ancestors, together with suitable coats
of arms.

True, Piper is not a name of much promise, but there
had been a Count Piper somewhere or other some
centuries ago, and the very rarity of the name proved
that every Piper must come from one common stock.
Fired by this generous idea, Mr. Cavendish gave himself
up to its pursuit with enthusiasm.   He would spend
whole hours in the Melbourne Library poring over books
of heraldry.   Every chronological or biographical docu-
ment bearing upon the age in which Count Piper was
supposed to have lived was made the subject of long and
minute examination.   When the monthly mail day came
round there would sure to be a budget of letters in
Mr. Cavendish's handwriting, addressed to the different
colleges and societies at home and abroad, who were to
help in extracting all Pipers of any importance from the
oblivion in which they had hitherto been suffered to
remain.

Mr. Piper is at length informed of the
progress of the inquiries, but shows a pro-
voking obtuseness and indifference concerning them.

'I am—hem!—I am pursuing a task of the utmost
consequence to your family interests,' Mr. Cavendish
had told him one day.   'In fact, my dear sir, I am
engaged in a work of no less moment than that of
reconstructing your family tree.'

'My what-do-you-call-it tree?' exclaimed Mr. Piper,

with a hazy idea that Mr. Cavendish had been trying some unwarrantable experiments upon his lemon and orange bushes. 'Don't you take and put any rubbish in the garden. I've got a new lot of guano, and I don't want it meddled with.'

'Guano !' echoed Mr. Cavendish, with a tone of the most withering compassion. 'I'm afraid you don't quite apprehend my meaning. I am not alluding to coarse material facts at all. I am speaking of a genealogical tree—a ge-ne-a-lo-gi-cal tree, you understand? I am trying to rescue your ancestors from the dust of oblivion. I am. . . .'

'You'd better leave 'em alone,' interrupted Mr. Piper, with the sulky accent of one whose suspicions have not been altogether allayed. '*They* won't do you any good —no more than they've done for me. You've got some of your own, I expect; that's enough for any man, I should think.'

Mr. Cavendish shrugged his shoulders and held his peace. If the matter had not become a hobby by this time, he would have abandoned it then and there. As it was, he contented himself by deploring the sad effects of low association upon the undoubted descendant of a count, and pondering upon the possibility of introducing a hog in armour instead of a stag at gaze into the coat-of-arms that he foresaw would be the result of his researches.

Equally comical is the spectacle of Mrs. Cavendish, on the eve of the first meeting of the two men, humbly wondering how she

could soften the heart of her discontented
lord towards the low-born brother—'how
lead him to pardon, as it were, his benefactor
for having dared to benefit him,' and the
subsequent reflection of Cavendish that not
only was wealth an acknowledged power,
'even though pork-sausages should have been
its alleged first cause,' but that, after all,
'politic members of the great ruling houses
in the old world had been known to make
concessions to trade,' and he 'was prepared
to make concessions too!' Accordingly, he
resolved that the meeting with his relative
should bear the semblance of cordiality.

'This is a real pleasure, my dear sir,' he said, with ten
white fingers — the fingers of thoroughbred hands—
closing round Mr. Piper's plebeian knuckles. No on-
looker could have supposed for an instant that he had
come, with the whole of his family, in an entirely desti-
tute condition, to live upon his wife's brother. Besides,
we know that among well-bred people, to receive a favour
is virtually to oblige a man. You only accept cordiali-
ties from people you esteem. . . .

'You're welcome, sir,' said Mr. Piper.

Then there was a pause, during which Mrs. Cavendish
wiped her eyes, and Mr. Piper said very heartily, 'You're
welcome, the lot of you.'

Cavendish is the only character that the author has treated in a consistently farcical vein. Eila Frost's canting old father-in-law in *Not Counting the Cost* is made ridiculous in his harangue on the duties of the young wife to her insane husband; but, with this exception, little is said of him in the story. It would seem that Tasma regards broadly humorous exaggeration to be scarcely compatible with her somewhat grave style, for in all the later stories her satire, if not less pungent, is of a quieter kind.

Next to their humour and skilful presentation of character, the most noteworthy feature of these novels is their lucid and polished language. The style is, perhaps, scarcely easy enough for fiction. Its qualities and culture are those that equip the essayist or critic rather than the novelist. Indeed, judged by some of her early work in the reviews, and by the little philosophic exordiums with which she opens so many of her chapters, Tasma would have made a brilliant essayist. To a large class of thoughtful readers it will always seem that what her novels lack in dramatic interest is fully compensated for by their more than usually faithful sketches of both men and women, and by their intimate and sympathetic view of our common life.

THE END.

BILLING AND SONS, PRINTERS, GUILDFORD.

G., C. & Co.

www.ingramcontent.com/pod-product-compliance
Lightning Source LLC
Chambersburg PA
CBHW020847020726
47497CB00005B/1301